'Raine proves his exc[ellent]... fluke, with this powerful and authentic tale of greed and revenge. His sparse prose means no words are wasted as he swiftly moves the grim – but often funny – story of high ambition and low achievement to an appropriately amoral conclusion. This is crime-writing at its very finest' *Crime Time*

'The trail of violence and black comedy unfolds in deceptively quiet prose that is remarkably revelatory without ever being judgemental. A gem of a book' Val McDermid, *Manchester Evening News*

'I loved it . . . shows that *Smalltime* was no one-off' Ian Rankin, *Crime Time*

'Acute, ironic study of suburban lowlife . . . where villainy is simply a case of going with the flow. A terrific follow-up to Raine's first novel. Quite exceptional' *Literary Review*

'Jerry Raine, whose *Smalltime* evoked an actute but accurate sense of south London and its downtrodden denizens, returns to the same bleak scene in *Frankie Bosser Comes Home*. A gentle surreal humour pervades this portrait of minor-league villains and criminal acquaintances going about their lives in neutral gear. A quiet, clever book about the sheer ordinariness of most criminal activities' *Time Out*

'The prose is tight and economical, but the effect he creates is one of poison and menace. Although grimly and all-too-believably realistic, Raine nevertheless imbues the book with a darkly surreal sense of humour. Brilliant' *Yorkshire Post*

Jerry Raine was born in Yorkshire, raised in East Africa and has also lived in Australia. In 1986 he won the *Mail on Sunday*'s fiction prize, and his first novel, *Smalltime*, was published in 1996. *Frankie Bosser Comes Home* is his second novel. *Slaphead Chameleon*, his third novel, is published by Victor Gollancz. Jerry Raine, who is also a singer/songwriter, currently lives in London.

By the same author

SMALLTIME
SLAPHEAD CHAMELEON

Frankie Bosser Comes Home

JERRY RAINE

ORION

An Orion paperback
First published in Great Britain by Victor Gollancz in 1999
This paperback edition published in 2000 by
Orion Books Ltd
Orion House, 5 Upper St Martin's Lane,
London WC2H 9EA

A CIP catalogue record for this book
is available from the British Library

ISBN 0 75283 438 X

Printed and bound in Great Britain by
Cox & Wyman Ltd, Reading, Berkshire

For Pam

1

The VW camper van pulled off the motorway at the Woodvale turn-off and Phil Gator climbed out. He hoisted his rucksack on to his shoulder and was ready to shut the door when the driver reached over with a joint in his hand.

'Here, one for the road,' he said, laughing and pushing his long dark hair away from his eyes.

Gator smiled and took the offering. He was already fairly stoned but one more wouldn't hurt.

'Thanks a lot,' he said. 'Mind how you drive.'

'I'm used to it,' the driver said. 'I'm on auto-pilot.'

Gator shut the door and watched the VW pull away, then reached in his jacket for a box of matches. He lit the joint and inhaled as he walked up the exit ramp.

It was a wet June afternoon but the rain had momentarily ceased after a violent thunderstorm about thirty minutes earlier. Luckily Gator had been inside the VW then and had been able to watch the rain through a haze of dope rather than being outside getting wet. It had taken him three lifts to hitch his way up from Dover, and now he was finally on the outskirts of his home town.

Walking with a spring in his step and enjoying the dope, Gator thought about his three months away from England. He'd been bumming his way through Spain and France, lying low after committing a robbery at a petrol station in a town a few miles away. With a stretch in prison three years before for an attempted robbery on a building society in Croydon, he had decided to clear out until things cooled down a little. He had walked out of his mechanic's job at a small garage in Horley, kissed his mother goodbye, then caught a train to the coast and the first available ferry. Now he was returning with a good tan, but with the dread of having to find a job and get back in the swing of things. His nine hundred pounds from the petrol station robbery was all gone.

When he reached the top of the exit ramp he turned left towards the hill that led down into Woodvale. Cars were circling the roundabout, either heading back down to the motorway or joining the slow queue into town. Woodvale had become a traffic bottleneck since the M25 had reached it some ten years before, but rather than add to the general well-being of the town it had only created new problems; Woodvale was now a town that people passed through rather than lingered in, and many of the shops in the centre had closed down. It was still a desirable place to live though, and there were many opulent homes in the surrounding areas owned by business types who commuted into London. As for Gator, his mother lived in a council house in one of the less fashionable streets.

At the top of Woodvale Hill Gator let his momentum take him down the slope. He was feeling tired from his hitching and also from the joints he'd been smoking. He was on a cigarette now, and he watched the rainwater in the gutter running down the hill. He passed a couple of pubs and hotels on his right, while on his left was countryside, the distant woods still showing gaps from the hurricane of 1987.

At the bottom of the hill the road flattened out as Gator approached the level crossing at Woodvale station. He noticed the rainwater had gathered in the drains, leaving large puddles by the side of the road, and moved over to the left so that passing cars wouldn't splash him.

He was coming to a sizeable puddle now and watched it closely as he approached. When he was right next to it a white van sped by as close to the kerb as it could get, and crashed through the water. Gator jumped sideways at the noise but it was too late. The water hit him like a tidal wave and soaked the whole of his right side: his jacket, his jeans, his rucksack and his trainers. The cigarette he'd been smoking was extinguished and he threw it in the gutter. He looked at the van as it drove on.

'You bastard!' he shouted, waving his fist.

He tried to brush the water from his clothes. Other cars were passing and he sensed the passengers smirking at him. He swore again and carried on walking. So that was the kind of welcome he got. Back in the country just a few hours and already the English population was showing him its pathetic sense of humour. He wished he were back in Spain lying on a beach.

His earlier drowsiness had now gone. As he carried on walking, he could feel his anger, and also a sense of despair, growing. Passers-by were looking at his wet trousers. Did they think he'd pissed himself?

There was no way it had been an accident because the puddle hadn't stretched into the middle of the road. The driver had had to drive right next to the kerb to make contact with it. So what was his problem? Gator had seen only one man in the van, so it wasn't as if he'd done it to get a laugh from a passenger. It was just a mean-bastard thing to do. He felt himself getting even angrier.

When he came to the Halfway House pub he turned left and starting walking down a road parallel to the railway line. On his left were some warehouses and another pub, imaginatively called the Railway. Gator walked past the smell of beer and glanced into the car park. He felt his pulse quicken when he saw the white van that had just splashed him parked there. And sitting inside, having a smoke, was the driver.

Gator marched into the car park and approached the van. As he got nearer he could see the man looking at him, a puzzled look coming on to his face. Gator took the rucksack off his right shoulder and dumped it by the front wheel. Then he walked to the driver's door and opened it.

'Thought that was pretty funny did you?' he snarled, pointing at his wet clothes. The driver looked at him blankly.

'What do you mean?' he said, cigarette smoke coming from his mouth and the cab. He was in his sixties, in dusty working trousers and a white T-shirt. He had a craggy red face, receding hair and the rough hands of a manual worker. Gator grabbed him by the T-shirt and pulled him on to the tarmac. The van-driver resisted but Gator had him standing in front of him in less than ten seconds. Although the man was slightly taller than him, Gator grabbed him by the throat and slammed him against the van. He liked the look of fear on the man's face.

'You should watch the way you drive, you know,' Gator said, in a voice so quiet the man hardly heard.

The man was just saying, 'What . . . ?' when Gator punched him hard in the face. The man's head snapped back and hit the van with a bang. Gator then hit him in the stomach, and as the man doubled over he kneed him on the chin. The man slid unconscious to the ground.

Gator picked up his rucksack and walked away. He could feel the strength surging through his arms. A small group of passers-by had gathered on the pavement and was watching him. They gave him disapproving looks as he walked away.

'What did you do that for?' a pensioner asked him.

Gator sneered and said, 'That's just the kind of bloke I am – if it's any of your business.'

He carried on walking and could hear their admonishing remarks behind him. He felt like turning round and swearing at them but decided it was best to leave it alone, and put some distance behind him before the cops turned up.

2

The man lying on the tarmac of the Railway was a sixty-one-year-old painter and decorator called Stanley. He had been driving home after finishing a job in Epsom that he'd been working on for two weeks. He came out of his unconscious state when someone poured a glass of water over his head. As he looked up from the ground he saw a gathering of people staring down, trying to get some words out of him.

'Are you OK, son?' someone asked. Stanley was so surprised at being called son he managed to get himself upright to look at the man asking the question. It was a little old guy who looked about a hundred.

'I'm OK,' Stanley said, and tried getting to his feet.

'Just stay there awhile – an ambulance is on its way,' someone else said.

'I don't need an ambulance,' Stanley said, struggling to his feet. He leaned against the van and decided he was well enough to drive. He was a proud man and hated having all these people looking at him.

'What was that all about?' the hundred-year-old guy asked.

'I haven't a clue,' Stanley replied.

'We got a good look at the boy,' an old lady said. 'We'll give a description when the police arrive.'

Stanley groaned to himself. The last thing he wanted was a question-and-answer session with the police. They would ask for his surname and a look of recognition would come into their eyes. They would give him knowing looks and be patronizing about things that had happened in the past; and they would

11

probably be quite glad that he'd been punched in the face. Then they would say they would do their best to catch the young man and would disappear in their cars, happy in the knowledge that maybe there was some justice in the world after all. No, Stanley could do without all that. He turned round and climbed into his van.

'You really shouldn't be driving,' a younger man said. He was dressed in a shirt and tie and looked like a waiter from the pub's restaurant.

'I'm OK, really,' Stanley said. 'I've been punched before. I'll get over it. Just tell the cops I won't be pressing charges.' He winked to show he was all right, turned the key in the ignition and slowly drove out of the car park.

Stanley lived in a detached four-bedroomed house, only five minutes away from where he'd been punched. He'd stopped in the Railway car park because he'd had a sudden attack of cramp in his right calf, a problem he seemed to be getting more and more these days. If it hadn't been for the intense pain, that young hooligan wouldn't have walked up to him and laid him out. As he drove his van up the driveway of his expensive home, he still hadn't figured out why he'd been punched.

He climbed out of the van and went indoors. He could hear his Italian wife Daniela in the kitchen, singing along to an awful pop song on the radio. He kissed her on the cheek and she asked him how his day had been. He said it had been pretty good until about ten minutes ago. When he told her about being punched, she came into his arms and stroked his face. She was a small woman with long dark hair.

'My poor Stanley,' she said. 'Why did this happen? Did you know the young man?'

'I've never seen him before,' Stanley said. 'Maybe he thought I was someone else. A case of mistaken identity. That sort of thing does happen.'

'Perhaps he just wanted to pick on someone and you were the first person he saw.'

'Maybe. I think I'm going to have a few bruises tomorrow.'

Daniela stroked his face some more. 'I'll run you a hot bath. Fix yourself a whisky – that will help.'

'Whisky is a good idea,' Stanley said, kissing his wife again.

He felt a lot better for seeing Daniela. She was only forty-five and they had been married for six years. Stanley had divorced his first wife nearly ten years ago, when he discovered she'd been having an affair with the next-door neighbour. He had punched the neighbour on the nose and his wife had run off with him. Afterwards Stanley hadn't been too proud about punching the neighbour, and maybe what had happened today was some kind of delayed payback. He believed that for anything bad you do in this life you get paid back somewhere down the line. Maybe today was it. He walked into the living room and fixed himself a large whisky and ginger ale from the drinks cabinet, and a gin and tonic for Daniela. Then he went back into the kitchen for ice.

Daniela came in from the bathroom and Stanley smiled at her.

'Your bath will be ready in five minutes,' she said.

He handed her the gin and tonic and they chinked their glasses.

'Here's to you,' Stanley said. 'The finest-looking woman I've ever known.'

Daniela laughed. 'No matter what happens you will always be a sweet talker,' she said.

After punching the man in the white van, Phil Gator had walked quickly along the road towards his mother's house. Within ten minutes he was in the small back garden, and reaching under a flowerpot for the back-door key. His mother was still at work and wouldn't be home for another few hours. She worked at the local swimming pool, sitting in a glass cubicle all day, taking entrance money from horrible schoolkids.

Gator's father had abandoned his wife and son when Phil was

13

still only a few months old. He had seen a photo of his father once: a big man standing outside a council house leaning on a bicycle. Gator didn't think about his dad too much and didn't subscribe to the view that his waywardness was due to his father's absence, an opinion several prison officials had given him in the past. As far as Gator was concerned he had turned out an OK citizen. He unlocked the back door and headed for his bedroom.

He walked slowly up the carpeted stairs and pushed open the bedroom door. The room was nicely tidied and ready for his return. The bed had clean sheets and when he pulled open the drawers of his only wardrobe, he saw clean underwear and socks, and T-shirts and jeans nicely ironed. God bless mothers! He chuckled and went to the bottom drawer of his bedside cabinet, pulled out his electric beard trimmer. Finding an old newspaper, he spread it on the floor in front of the wardrobe mirror, and stripped off until he was completely naked.

He put a chair on top of the newspaper and, using a small hand mirror so he could see the back of his head, started shaving off his long blond hair, which hadn't been cut for about six months. He was quite expert at cutting his own hair and hadn't been to a barber's since coming out of prison three years before. He hated sitting in a barber's chair making inane conversation, preferring to let his hair grow long and then cutting it all off himself.

Fifteen minutes later he was staring at his close crop. He brushed the loose hair off his shoulders, rolled the newspaper into a ball and put it at the top of the stairs. Then he grabbed a towel and walked along the hall to the bathroom.

He stood under the shower for a long time, soaping himself well and getting rid of the smells of the last five days on the road. He had only showered occasionally on his trip abroad and it would be nice to bathe regularly again. He believed in the body beautiful and thought his was one of the finest. He had strong arms and wide shoulders from six months of pumping iron in prison, and his mechanic's job had kept him fit since. When he'd

14

finished, he wiped the steam from the mirror above the sink, and dug out one of his old razors.

He shaved the five-day stubble from his cheeks and left himself a goatee beard. The image in front of him now was totally different from the long-haired traveller who had hit the man in the car park. The small group of passers-by could give whatever description they liked to the police; it would look nothing like the cropped tough guy now standing before the bathroom mirror.

After getting dressed in a clean pair of jeans and T-shirt, Gator picked up the ball of newspaper and went down to the kitchen where he stuffed it at the bottom of the waste bin. He put on a pair of boots, grabbed his leather jacket, and went out of the back door.

Sauntering along the residential street, he felt quite pleased with himself. He always felt fresh after cutting off all his hair and it was a nice day to be out, the sun returning to the sky after the earlier downpour. It didn't take him long to walk to the swimming pool, and when he pushed his way through the revolving door, there was his mother sitting in the glass cubicle. She looked up at him and smiled, and he smiled back.

'Hi, Mum, I'm home,' he said.

Lying in a steaming bath, with another stiff whisky sitting on the edge, Stanley was still trying to figure out why he had been punched. He went back through the events of the last few weeks and couldn't think of a single person he'd upset; he was not the sort of man to upset people. He was easy-going, loved his work, loved his wife, tried to get through each day without making waves. The bit of trouble he'd had in the past was well forgotten by most people, except the local police and some of his neighbours who still gave him snooty looks. But he hadn't been charged with anything back then and he hadn't been directly involved in anything bad; he had only been taking care of his son, who had got himself in a whole load of trouble.

No, Stanley couldn't think of a single thing.

He held his breath and ducked under the soapy water. Then a light went on in his head and he remembered that the young man who'd hit him had wet clothes when he'd approached the van. Stanley came out of the water, his heart beating a little faster. He remembered back to the drive down Woodvale Hill when he'd had the attack of cramp in his right calf. The sudden pain had made him veer sharply to the left side of the road, and, yes, now he remembered crashing through a large puddle when someone had been standing right next to it. It must have been the young man, and his wet clothes must have been caused by Stanley. But surely that was no reason to go punching someone's lights out. Unless the young man was some kind of a nutter to begin with.

The more Stanley thought about it, the more he figured this was what had happened. He felt himself tensing, getting angry, hoping he would bump into the young man again someday. And this time he would be ready for him.

He felt a twinge of cramp coming into his right calf again and reached down to pull his toes towards him to relieve it. As he did, he also felt a slight tingling along his right arm. He leaned back into the water and found himself struggling to breathe. What the hell is happening now? he thought. He closed his eyes and tried to relax until the pain went.

About thirty minutes later Daniela left the food she was preparing and went along to the bathroom to see how Stanley was doing. She opened the door and thought her husband was merely asleep when she saw him lying there looking relaxed. It was only when she tried to wake him that she realized her worst nightmare had come true. She ran into the hall and telephoned for an ambulance.

While she waited she went back into the bathroom and sat on the edge of the bath. She started to weep, and stroked Stanley's forehead. Then she pulled herself together, got up, went into the living room and picked up the telephone. She dialled a number in Italy and when the call was answered she could hear the noise in the bar where Stanley's son worked. Daniela spoke in Italian to a waitress. She asked to speak to her stepson and the waitress requested her name.

Daniela said, 'Tell him it's Daniela Bosser. And tell him it's urgent.'

3

In another part of Woodvale, Jason Campbell was sitting by the telephone waiting for it to ring. A few weeks before he had put an advert in the local paper for a lodger to share his house, and he was getting desperate for someone decent to reply. In the past week he'd received phone calls from one unemployed person, a recovering alcoholic, a sixty-year-old retired bus driver and a freelance photographer who needed a large house to take snaps of semi-naked girls. He hadn't asked any of them to come round to view his place and was wondering if this was the best that was on offer in Woodvale, this so-called respectable commuter town in Surrey. Surely not.

The ideal lodger as far as Jason was concerned was a professional person who had to work all hours so he was hardly ever at home. But he supposed that would be asking far too much.

Jason took a sip from his glass of chilled white wine. He was watching *Single White Female* on video. It was an entertaining film about the flatmate from hell, the psycho that comes to share the home of a yuppie working girl. Jason knew there could be problems with renting out part of his house, but convinced himself that things like this didn't happen in real life. The first priority was to get someone who could afford the rent, and if that person also turned out to be compatible too, then all well and good.

He had bought the three-bedroomed house with his girlfriend, Heather, just over five years earlier. They had split up six months ago, Heather getting sick and tired of the meagre living he had been scratching out as a guitar teacher and musician. Their mortgage had been £550 a month, and Jason had been contributing about £200 of that, while Heather had been paying the rest, plus all their food and bills. Jason couldn't blame Heather for leaving, but he wished she had stuck it out. After all, they had been together for over six years, so she knew well enough how much money he earned. Maybe there were other, deeper reasons for her leaving, and she had just used the money issue as the easiest option. Jason had always thought Heather would be tough enough to hang in there with him, but obviously not. She had moved into a rented flat in London to be closer to work, and no doubt to hang out with some high-flyers with a thirty-grand income. He now knew that the saying 'When the going gets tough the tough get going' was perfectly true. They go and leave you to deal with the shit on your own.

The telephone rang.

Jason nearly dropped his glass of wine but recovered in time to set it on the carpet. He put the video on pause and picked up the receiver.

'Hello?' he said.

'I'm ringing about the room. Is it still available?' A man's voice.

'Yes, it's still available,' Jason said.

'Good. I was wondering whether you had a garage as well. I've got a couple of cars and I need somewhere to park them.'

'A couple of cars?'

'Well, actually, four at the moment. I buy and sell second-hand cars so I need plenty of space to park them.'

Jason took a deep breath. Was the whole world going mad?

'You've got four cars and you want to park them all in my drive and my garage?'

'It'll only be temporary of course. I'll be selling two of them fairly quickly.'

'And then you'll be buying more, no doubt.'

'Well, maybe.'

'Sounds like definitely to me.'

'Well, that is how I make my living.'

'I'm sorry, mate,' Jason said, 'but I think you need to rent a garage not a room. I have a car myself and that's the only vehicle I want on my premises. One more I could handle but not four.'

'I can pay extra for the cars.'

The word 'extra' rang like a bell in Jason's head. Extra would be really handy at the moment.

'How much extra?' he asked cagily.

'You name the price,' the man said. 'It's up to you. Maybe I could come round for a chat?'

Jason thought for a few seconds. He would have to start seeing prospective boarders eventually. He couldn't keep turning everyone down on the phone. 'OK,' he said, trying to summon up some enthusiasm.

He gave the man his address and the man said, 'My name's Karl, by the way. Karl with a K. I'll be there in a mo.' And the line went dead.

Jason hung up and wondered what he was getting himself into. Was he really going to rent out a room and his drive to a second-hand car dealer? Was he really as desperate as that? He thought that maybe he was. He needed to get some money rolling in. He finished his glass of wine and thought he'd better sober up a little before the guy turned up. How long had he said? A mo. How long was a mo?

Jason went to the kitchen, set his glass by the sink and put the rest of the wine in the fridge. Then he stood in front of the washbasin in the downstairs toilet, and took off his glasses. He splashed some cold water on his face, dried himself on a hand towel and inspected his medium-length dark hair in the mirror. He seemed to be getting a few extra grey hairs every day. Still, he was pretty good-looking for thirty-nine, and with more money rolling in could even think about dating again.

He went back to the living room and looked out at the front garden. It had a small patch of lawn and a hedge, which was looking a bit raggedy as Jason hated going out there with his shears to trim it every month. His fingers could fly across the fretboard of a guitar but they weren't green, and in the past the gardening had all been taken care of by Heather. Jason would have to deal with the back garden as well, which was at least ten times bigger than the little square he was looking at now. Maybe this Karl would turn out to be a prize gardener as well as a second-hand car dealer. Jason doubted it somehow.

His doubts increased when he saw a car roll up and a tough-looking guy with a goatee climb out. He had short-cropped hair and a head the shape of an egg. He was looking up at the house, inspecting, and then he stared straight at Jason, who felt the force of that look almost physically and stepped back one pace in shock. He glanced at his watch and saw that a 'mo' had been about twelve minutes.

Jason went to open the front door. Karl was grinning as he pushed at the garden gate, and Jason gave him the once-over as he walked up the path. He was about six foot two, had slightly bowed legs, wide sloping shoulders, and was wearing jeans and Doc Martens. He had on a shrunken black T-shirt, so small that his midriff was showing: a flat, tanned stomach that looked as hard as a wooden table. He marched forward and held out a big hand to be shaken. Jason grasped it tentatively, thinking about his guitar-playing future as his hand went into what he expected would be a crusher. But he was surprised to find the handshake very limp, almost ladylike. Was that even more worrying?

'Karl Spoiler's my name, and second-hand cars are my game,' the man said, laughing. Jason noticed up close that he had one completely silver tooth on the left side of his mouth, about four in from the middle. He also had a silver earring in his left ear.

'I'm Jason Campbell. Pleased to meet you.' It didn't sound convincing, even to Jason.

'Nice house you have here,' Karl said. 'This would really be ideal for me.' He looked at the garden and surrounding area, taking it all in. And then he was off, walking to the side of the house and the drive. He turned back to Jason and pointed to the rear of the house. 'Can I look in the garage?' he asked innocently.

Jason picked up the keys from the hall table and walked round to the detached garage. He unlocked it and pulled up the door. Inside sat his little red Mini, with the usual garage clutter scattered around the walls and workbench.

Karl was nodding. 'Nice size,' he said. 'Nice size.'

Jason watched Karl as he wandered round the garage, nosing about, looking at his tools, then looking at the Mini.

'Good condition,' Karl said. 'Had it long?'

'A few years,' Jason said. 'It belongs to my girlfriend. Or ex-girlfriend. She's gone to live in London, so she said I could have it for a while. She says she doesn't need it up there.'

'Tubes,' Karl said.

'Pardon?'

'Tubes,' Karl repeated. 'You don't really need a car in London with the Underground.'

Jason nodded. He had never lived in London and didn't wish to. He had always lived in Surrey, in various towns, and never saw the appeal of the Smoke, although he played about two gigs a week up there on average. Driving in on those occasions was about all the excitement he needed. Heather had also always lived in Surrey, but apparently was now loving the big city life. He wondered if she was seeing anyone else yet.

Karl bent down, looking under the Mini, prodding away with his hands. 'No sign of rust,' he said. 'If you ever want to sell her I could get you a good price.'

'I can't sell her,' Jason said. 'It's up to Heather.'

'Heather's your ex, you said?'

'Yeah.'

'Unusual name.'

'Not really.'

'Makes me think of foliage.'

Jason was surprised Karl even knew the word foliage.

Karl came out of the garage. 'Can I see the rest of the place?'

Jason showed him the back garden first; the lawn needed cutting again; the flower beds needed weeding. Karl didn't mention anything about an interest in gardening so Jason dismissed his earlier hopes. There was a patio at the back of the house, where Jason spent many idle afternoons reading, and at the side near the garage a few steps led to the basement door. He walked down, unlocked it, and took Karl into the basement and turned on the light.

'Wow!' Karl said, as they walked in. 'Now this is very nice.'

The basement was almost the size of the whole ground floor, and was situated under the kitchen, living room and hall. Jason used it as his studio and teaching room. He had a small thirty-five-watt amp, one electric and three acoustic guitars, a microphone, an electric piano and music stands for when he was teaching. The basement was surprisingly damp-free, and had one radiator for the winter. It was the potential of this area that had first persuaded Jason to buy the house. He spent most of his free hours down here, and could make as much noise as he wanted without disturbing the neighbours. The acoustics were superb.

'Are you a musician?' asked Karl.

'Sort of,' Jason said. 'I teach guitar during the day and in the evenings, and play the occasional gig in London. I'm not making enough money at the moment, though. That's why I need a lodger.'

'Well, I make plenty of money,' Karl said.

Jason waited for him to elaborate but Karl just continued looking round the basement.

'Where are you living at the moment?' Jason asked.

'I've been living with this bloke in Redgate. But he recently met a Spanish girl and now the Spanish girl is going to move in with him. So it's bye-bye, Karl. I think they're going to get married. The bloke also didn't like having my cars around. Spoiled the general landscape, he said. I don't see the problem with four cars myself. I mean, most families seem to have that many cars, what with their kids driving.'

'There are far too many cars in the world,' Jason said.

'I agree, but if I can buy and sell 'em, who am I to argue?'

'And you make decent money out of it?'

'More than decent,' Karl said proudly. 'It's something I know how to do, and I do it well.'

'So where do your parents live?'

'They're down in Ramsgate,' Karl said. 'With my two brothers. I left home when I was eighteen.'

Jason's parents lived in Bristol. He saw them about twice a year and his older sister even less. 'How old are you now?' he asked.

'Twenty-four.'

'Don't you miss them? I would quite like living by the sea.'

'Yeah, anyone who hasn't lived by the sea says that. But I say fuck the sea. It's so windy down there. Wherever you walk you feel like someone's trying to hold you back. And tourists. Too many of the buggers.'

It was time to bring up the money question. 'So how much extra would you be willing to pay for your cars?' Jason asked.

Karl looked at him seriously. 'I was reckoning on, say, twenty pounds per car. So if there's four cars, I pay you an extra eighty pounds a month. That comes to three-eighty a month in total.'

The pound signs were ringing up in Jason's head. He could see his worries disappearing in one swift moment. 'Sounds fair enough,' he said. 'There's a three-hundred-pound deposit too, though, then one month's rent in advance, plus a share of the bills.'

'Don't worry about it,' Karl said. 'I have it all here.'

He reached in his jeans pocket and pulled out a wad of money: all pink fifty-pound notes. Jason watched Karl count them out.

'I have seven hundred pounds right here,' Karl said. 'It's all yours. You can owe me the twenty quid.'

Jason wanted to grab the money right away, run down to the bank and wipe out his overdraft. Instead he said, 'You'd better see the rest of the house first.'

About thirty minutes later Karl was walking away from the house with a key in his hand. Jason was standing by the front door with seven hundred pounds in his pocket. He felt a bit nervous about the thought of living with Karl, but what the hell, he was nearly forty years old, he was a big boy now. If there were any problems he would just ask Karl to leave. The important thing was that he had his money, and that would solve his immediate problems. And, anyway, Karl seemed fairly normal compared to the other people who had been ringing him up the past few weeks.

After leaving the basement, Jason had taken Karl upstairs and shown him what would now be his room. He had decided to give the large bedroom to whoever came around, and take one of the small back bedrooms himself. He never spent any time upstairs anyway. He only needed somewhere to sleep.

Karl had been very happy at the size of his new room. It looked out over the front garden and street, had a double bed, two wardrobes and two chests of drawers. He had eyed the double bed with glee and had asked about bringing women back. Jason had said he didn't really mind, as long as it didn't get in the way of his teaching. He didn't want scantily clad women running around if he had a pupil in his house. Karl agreed to that. No scantily clad women except in his room.

Next they had walked to the drive and figured out how many cars would reasonably fit there. With one in the garage and two in the drive, that would only leave two on the street, which was pretty normal. Jason wondered why he had been so worried about it. He had been worrying too much about his neighbours as usual. Well, fuck them. It was his house and his property, and he could use it any way he wanted. There was nothing that said he couldn't have a load of cars around.

He watched Karl's head disappear behind the front hedge as he climbed into his car. Then he went back to the fridge and fetched his bottle of wine. He poured a celebratory glass and toasted himself.

'Goodbye money problems,' he said out loud. 'Hello Easy Street.'

He sipped the wine, but it had gone a little sour.

4

In the Italian ski resort of Courmayeur, Frankie Bosser was getting ready to leave. He picked up his suitcase, left his bedroom and walked down the narrow wooden stairs into Mike's Bar. Mike was cleaning up behind the counter, getting ready for the day to begin.

'You're ready to leave?' he asked.

'Yeah. Have you seen Veronica?'

'She's outside with the car, waiting for you.'

'Right. I'd better get going.'

'Good luck. Take as long as you want. We're not too busy at the moment.'

'Thanks.'

They shook hands.

Frankie opened the outside door and walked down the stone steps. Veronica was sitting in her red Alfa Romeo, the engine running. Frankie opened the boot, dropped in his suitcase, then climbed in the passenger seat. Veronica was wearing a very short skirt, showing lots of leg in black tights, and he smiled at her as he fastened his seat belt.

'Not for you,' she said, in Italian. 'Not for you.'

Frankie smiled and squeezed her on the knee.

Veronica drove slowly down the narrow cobbled street and then turned on to the main road. She switched on the radio and hummed along to a pop tune.

'I'm going to get some sleep,' Frankie said. 'I didn't get much last night.'

'You sleep,' Veronica said. 'You were always falling asleep on me, anyway.'

Frankie chuckled and tilted the seat back a bit. He laid his head on the headrest and closed his eyes.

His restless night had come after the telephone call from Daniela. He had felt a deep sadness and loss when she'd told him about his father. He had also felt helpless, and extremely depressed that he was stranded in a different country. He hadn't seen his father for over three years, and now he had been robbed of him. He had cursed himself for the bad luck that had forced him to leave England, and for the things he had never said to his father, the things his father would now never know or hear.

After receiving the bad news, Frankie had gone up to his room and fought the inclination to have a stiff drink. He had given up drinking on arrival in Courmayeur as a penance for his previous life in England. Mike had chatted to him for about an hour, sharing his own feelings about when both his parents had been killed in a car crash over ten years before. When Mike had left the room Frankie had put on a tracksuit and gone jogging for nearly an hour. Although Courmayeur was a ski resort, the roads were always clear of snow and jogging was no problem. Eventually, he had felt tired enough to return to the bar, and had fallen asleep in his armchair. Now he was trying to sleep in another kind of seat, and then he would make a third attempt on the aeroplane.

As he dozed Frankie thought about the consequences of going back to England. It was a risk – and he was travelling with a false passport – but he knew he couldn't miss the funeral of his father, the man who had put himself on the line for him three years ago so he could get away from England. This was the least he could do. If the cops caught up with him this time, then that would just be tough shit and he would have to pay the price. He could never live with himself if he played the coward and missed seeing his father for one last time.

And things had been going so well up to now.

After fleeing England Frankie had gone to Courmayeur and lodged at Mike's Bar. His stepmother Daniela had contacts in

Courmayeur, and had arranged the whole thing. Frankie had helped out in the bar in the evenings and had learned to ski during the day. He had become an expert skier over the three years, and now worked full time in the bar. He had also bought a few shares in the place to give him more incentive to stay. Mike had never asked too many questions about Frankie's sudden appearance, and Frankie had always appreciated that. The simple village life, looking after skiers in the winter and older tourists in the summer, was a welcome change after the uncertainty and excitement of his life in England.

Mike was a tall, thin Englishman with a ruddy face, a former alcoholic who had been off the bottle for about eight years. He had originally gone to Courmayeur to ski, had fallen in love with the place, and had never returned to England. After years of working behind various bars, and giving private skiing lessons to holidaying Britons and Americans, he had saved enough to buy a share in a bar. The bar had an excellent location, right in the middle of Courmayeur's cobblestoned main street, but had never taken much money. Mike suggested changing the name, and immediately it became the major place for Britons and Americans to meet. He also threw out all the old seating and replaced it with armchairs and sofas, so the bar now had the feel of someone's living room, with log fires and English landscape paintings on the walls. As business picked up the Italian owners let him buy a bigger share in the business, and became sleeping partners. They preferred staying at home looking after their grandchildren rather than worrying about rich tourists. Mike ran the bar with three Italian waitresses, had a chef preparing bar food, and now had Frankie as an extra barman and occasional bouncer.

The car jerked and Frankie opened his eyes. He looked over at Veronica who looked back and winked. Frankie closed his eyes. They had had a brief affair when Frankie first arrived in Courmayeur, but were now just good, close friends. Veronica was tall and slim, with straight dark hair. She was the best-looking waitress at Mike's and got asked out by tourists virtually every night. They had ended up in bed together one evening after Veronica had drunk too much, but after several similar couplings had decided to call it quits. It was too much strain to go out with someone you worked with. Frankie still got jealous whenever he saw Veronica with a man on her arm, but he would never do anything about it as long as he was at Mike's Bar. Besides, he liked to have a few flings himself.

After falling into a deep sleep for half an hour or so, Frankie awoke to find they were getting close to Milan. He chatted to Veronica about work until she pulled up at the airport to let him out.

'Have a good trip, Frankie,' she said. 'It will be good for you to go home, despite what's happened.'

Frankie nodded. 'It'll be nice to see the home town. I'll miss you, though.' He leaned over to kiss her on the cheek.

'And I'll miss you,' she said. 'I'll leave lots of dirty glasses for you!'

Frankie laughed. He looked into her dark eyes and kissed her again. Maybe when he came back he should forget his inhibitions and get serious with her. Or maybe he was just feeling sentimental because of his predicament. He climbed out and got his suitcase from the boot. He waved as he walked away. Veronica blew him a kiss.

Getting on the plane for Gatwick was no problem with his false passport, but Frankie had plenty of cold sweats on the flight, thinking about what might happen when they landed. He would just have to play it cool, walk through customs like any other holidaymaker returning home.

He tried to sleep again, but sleeping on planes was impossible. He thought back to the last time he had seen his father . . .

On that fateful night over three years ago Frankie had turned up at his father's house in Woodvale in a state of panic. He had just shot a man who had been snooping in the garden of his house, and after searching through the man's clothes had been

29

astonished to discover he was a policeman. It had been an accident, of course, but Frankie knew he would have to leave the country fast. He drove up to Woodvale to see his father and Daniela, after hiding the policeman's body in the woods at the back of his house.

After hearing the bad news Frankie's father suggested he turn himself in. He reminded him about the case a few years ago when a villain called Kenny Boyce had shot an undercover policeman in his garden and got away with it because the policeman shouldn't have been there anyway. Frankie had told his father that Boyce could afford good lawyers and it wasn't a chance he wanted to take. He would leave the country first and watch the situation from a distance. His father reluctantly agreed, and offered to drive him to the coast for a hovercraft to France first thing in the morning. Daniela made phone calls to friends in Courmayeur, and Frankie was all set.

On the drive down to Dover in the early hours Frankie told his father what to do about his business and employees while he was away. He wrote down phone numbers of people to contact to wind things down.

Frankie was a self-employed importer of alcohol from France, and had been doing very nicely at it for about thirteen years. Before that he had been a sales representative for a card company, his first respectable job after spending most of his youth working in local factories. He had packed in the salesman job at the age of twenty-eight, after tiring of the constant driving around Britain, the nights in cheap hotels, the daily wearing of suits and the false smiles he had to give customers for whom he had no respect.

His life had changed innocently enough. On a day trip to France he had brought a load of drink back in the boot of his car and then sold it in England for a tidy profit. Soon after, he packed in his sales job and started making regular trips across the Channel.

He rented a cottage in the village of Burmarsh near Folkestone to be close to the coast. Then he bought a Volkswagen van, and started making two or three trips a week. He would then sell on the booze: to pubs, nightclubs, social clubs and to friends and acquaintances from his card-selling days. Soon he was making more money than he had been as a rep, and after six months had to take on his first employee.

As the business grew over the years, Frankie employed two more people, bought three Sherpa vans, and had twelve different bank accounts to hide his money. His annual turnover exceeded a hundred thousand pounds, and he employed a crooked accountant called Malcolm to keep track of everything and to hold the Inland Revenue at bay. As his reputation grew he became known as Frankie Boozer.

The 'Eurobooze' scam, as it soon became known, was so easy that eventually everyone was doing it; organized crime moved in and Frankie decided it was time to rethink his operation. As competition grew the gangs of importers started using force to get landlords and club owners to take their drink. Frankie hadn't wanted to get involved in anything heavy and realized the honeymoon period was over.

He scaled his business down, keeping it going, but adopting a low profile as a safe option. Competitors were starting to get arrested, and another major importer was taken in after Customs put him under surveillance. Frankie didn't want to be the next target.

A little while later Frankie started getting anonymous letters, telling him that he should clear his business out of Burmarsh or something bad would happen. He had laughed it off at first as just an irate local wanting to keep the village peaceful, but when the letters continued he had bought himself a shotgun just to be safe. Then, when he shot the policeman that night, he figured that maybe it was the policeman who had been sending him the letters, trying to harass him and drive him out of town. The policeman had only been a constable, so maybe he was trying to further his career, get a leg up the ladder of promotion. Frankie had never found out for sure and would never know now.

When Frankie and his father arrived at Dover, they had waited nervously for the hovercraft, neither of them knowing what to say. After a quick, compassionate hug, Frankie was on his way. He travelled by train to Italy, arriving in Courmayeur two days later.

As Frankie walked towards passport control at Gatwick he took deep breaths to relax. His false passport carried the name of Terry Elliott, an English skier he had befriended one evening the previous December. Skiers were always keen to mix with the locals, but Frankie usually kept his distance unless they were pretty girls or, as in the case of Terry, someone he could get something out of. It hadn't taken Frankie more than a minute to realize that, without his beard, Terry would look a lot like himself. Ever since arriving in Courmayeur, Frankie had known he would one day have to find a false passport, and this seemed like the ideal opportunity. He had hung out with Terry and his group of drunken friends for a few evenings, found out the hotel and room where Terry was staying and stolen his passport one morning when the maids were doing their cleaning rounds.

The picture in Terry's passport showed him with his beard, and short hair the same length as Frankie's and almost the same colour, although Frankie was more blond. For the cursory glance that bored passport controllers used, Frankie could quite easily be Terry.

As the line edged closer to the passport desk, Frankie wiped the sweat from his forehead. When his turn came he handed over the passport, and two seconds later it was being handed back to him. He looked up in surprise but the controller was already looking at the next person in line. Frankie walked on. He had made it through! He felt like jumping in the air and clicking his heels.

After picking up his suitcase Frankie walked outside and joined the queue for taxis. Daniela had volunteered to meet him, but Frankie had declined the offer in case he ran into any difficulties.

'I need the Station Hotel in Redgate,' Frankie said as he climbed in the next available cab. He made sure he was sitting diagonally behind the driver, out of sight of the rearview mirror. The driver nodded.

'Business or pleasure?' the driver asked when they were out of the airport and on the dual carriageway.

'Neither,' Frankie said. He watched the driver look in his mirror, knowing he could not be seen. 'Well, pleasure, I suppose,' he added. 'I've come for the wedding of a friend. Flown over from Spain. I don't really like weddings, so there's not much pleasure in it for me. More a sense of duty.' Frankie was such a practised liar he was never surprised at the stories he could think up on the spur of the moment.

'I know what you mean,' the driver said. 'Most people think weddings are fun, but they can be depressing as well. Usually if you've been unlucky in love.'

'That's me.' Frankie chuckled.

'Me too,' the driver said. 'Give me a good funeral any day. A truly uplifting experience.'

Frankie didn't think his father's funeral would be particularly uplifting but he smiled anyway, the good-natured traveller returning to his home country.

They made more small talk as Frankie looked out of the window at pubs he had frequented as a teenager. Nothing much ever changed in this particular part of Surrey and he guessed that was part of the appeal it held for most people. After being brought up in a small village called Nutfield, Frankie had lived most of his youth in Woodvale and its neighbouring town of Redgate, and had only moved away from the area when he'd got the sales rep job. He knew this place like the back of his hand, and supposed it was his real home. It was nice to see it again after such a long break.

Soon they were driving into Redgate, around the one-way system that skirted the large indoor shopping centre, then past the station and under the railway bridge to the Station Hotel. Daniela had already made a reservation for him. Frankie didn't want to stay at his father's house. It would be too risky. He was sure the local cops would be keeping an eye out for him.

He gave the taxi driver a generous tip and walked to the hotel's main door. As a teenager he'd been drinking here more times than he cared to remember, and when he walked into the lobby he discovered it was the same as ever. He checked in, still using the name of Terry Elliott. He took his key and walked up the carpeted stairs to his room.

The room looked out over the front of the hotel and the main road. It was the standard hotel room: single bed, chest of drawers, wardrobe, attached bathroom – no shower – trouser press and TV. Across the road was the Home Cottage pub, Frankie's favourite haunt from his youth. When he left school at the age of sixteen he had worked in the Fuller's Earth factory about a mile up the road. The factory-workers would go drinking in the Home Cottage between shifts, and after a few pints cross over to the Station Hotel if nothing was happening. Or sometimes the other way round. It had been a happy, carefree period of his life, bouncing from bar to bar, earning good money in the factory and sleeping in a cheap, grotty bedsit.

In the Station Hotel there was a big ballroom downstairs and on Thursday nights a band and a succession of local singers would do their turns. Frankie remembered one of the blokes he had worked with at Fuller's Earth, a quiet chap whose name he couldn't remember, who sang and played guitar. He would get up on stage on Thursday nights and sing folk songs in a loud, clear voice, while Frankie and a few others from the factory looked on. They would cheer loudly at the end of each song and then make their way up the road for the night shift. They were good times, and Frankie felt a little depressed thinking about them now.

He walked to the bed, opened his suitcase, took out a pack of cigarettes and lit one up. Although he had turned into something of a fitness freak since giving up drinking, he was still puffing away on the old coffin nails. Well, you couldn't give up everything, could you? Then he went to the telephone and dialled Daniela's number. She picked it up on the third ring.

'The prodigal son returns,' Frankie said, and took another drag on his cigarette.

5

In the Red Lion pub, just over the road from Woodvale Police Station, Detective Inspector Jesse Morgan was sitting at a table listening to Detective Sergeant Ian Kiddie. It was Thursday lunchtime, and Morgan was glad to be away from his office, another uneventful six-to-two shift having just finished for both of them.

The pub was quiet, filled mainly with older people. Youngsters tended to avoid it because they knew it was always full of policemen.

Kiddie was a tall Scotsman, with ginger hair and moustache, pale skin and a red nose. He was from Dundee originally and still had a strong accent despite living in England for over ten years.

'So we get to the Railway – ' Kiddie was saying ' – that's me and Brazier. And there's this group of pensioners, and they say the victim has vanished. He's got into his van and driven away.'

'The man who was hit?' asked Morgan.

'Yeah. A guy in his sixties. Receding grey hair. Some sort of builder. He was driving a van and was wearing working clothes.'

Kiddie paused and took a large bite from a cheese roll. Morgan sipped on his half-pint and wondered where this was leading. Kiddie could talk most people into the ground, and this could be another of those occasions. Sometimes they would sit in the pub after work for a few hours, and on walking out Morgan would be unable to recall what the hell they had been talking about all evening. But Morgan was the patient type, and he supposed Kiddie was his best friend. He would indulge him before going back to the office to finish some after-hours paperwork. He always felt at a loss when the morning shift ended as he didn't have any social life in Woodvale. Invariably he would just catch up on paperwork when the shift finished so there wasn't such a long afternoon stretching ahead of him when he went home. It was a situation that depressed him more than a little, but he was hopeful it might change soon.

'So we took a few statements,' Kiddie continued, 'and went on our merry way.'

'And then what?'

'The next day we get a call from the coroner's office about a man who died the same day. The man's doctor said the man had died of a heart attack, but there may have been suspicious circumstances. There was a slight bruise on the man's forehead and left cheek, and other bruises on his ribs. The doctor called the coroner, the coroner went to have a look and then called me.'

'And the coroner agreed?'

Kiddie nodded. 'He thinks the man died from a heart attack but suspects it was trauma related.'

Morgan took another sip of beer and glanced over at the bar. The real reason he came in here most lunchtimes was standing there now. She was called Nicola and he thought she was one of the best-looking women he had ever seen. She saw him, made a gun with her right hand and shot him through the heart. Morgan clutched his chest and smiled at her as she blew the tips of her fingers. One day he would ask her out. He knew she was single and guessed she was at least ten years younger than his forty-six. But you didn't get anywhere in this world without trying.

'So, the doctor', Kiddie carried on, 'tells the man's wife that he can't issue a death certificate until there's been a coroner's inquiry. The wife goes loopy and they have a big row. She says they have to bury her husband because his son is flying back from Europe for the funeral. Now I'll drop you the first hint.'

'I thought we'd get to it eventually,' Morgan said.

'The wife is Italian and her husband's name is Bosser.'

Morgan looked at him blankly. The name meant nothing to him. 'You have to remember,' he said, 'that I've only been in the

37

area for just over a year. I don't know the history of the place. The name Bosser means nothing to me.'

Kiddie held up his hand in apology. 'I forgot. Well, as this is going to be a long story, let me buy you another drink.'

'How about you give me the money and I'll go up and get them?'

'OK,' Kiddie said. He reached in his pocket and came out with a handful of one-pound coins. He dropped them on the table and Morgan went up to see Nicola. He ordered two more half-pints of bitter.

'Drinking on duty again?' Nicola teased.

One of the reasons Nicola was tugging Morgan's heartstrings was that she reminded him of a girl he had gone out with at school, who by a major coincidence was also called Nicola. The Nicola in front of him now had the same short, dark hair, the same shape of face, the same slim figure. Morgan found it unsettling that someone he last saw over thirty years ago could still come back to haunt him in the form of another woman. Such was the power of love. Or was it obsession?

'I've finished for the day,' Morgan said. 'Another action-packed shift in Woodvale has already drawn to a close.'

Nicola smiled at him as she pulled on the pumps. 'I thought being a policeman was an exciting life.'

'Not these days it isn't. The more I get promoted the less exciting it becomes.'

'You could always do something bad and get demoted.' Nicola winked and placed the two drinks on the bar. Was that reply loaded with double meaning? Morgan smiled uneasily and gave her three of Kiddie's pound coins.

'You probably get more excitement in here,' he said when she had her back to him, ringing the amount into the till. He couldn't stop his eyes from straying down her body. She was wearing black slacks and trainers.

'You must be joking,' Nicola laughed. 'There's so many of you lot dropping in this must be the safest pub in town.'

'That's what we're here for.'

'And all the villains drink elsewhere.'

'You know those places, do you?'

'I might.'

'You'll have to show me some time.'

Nicola held out the change and put it into his hand. Morgan liked the touch of her fingers. It made his head feel momentarily dizzy. Or was that the beer?

'When?' asked Nicola.

But before Morgan could answer, Kiddie was standing next to him reaching for his beer.

'I need some nuts as well,' Kiddie said to Nicola.

Morgan looked angrily at Kiddie. Now the moment was gone. A golden opportunity to fix a date with Nicola. He had to walk back to the table to calm down before he gave Kiddie his own special brand of nuts – bruised from a hefty kick courtesy of his right boot.

When Kiddie reached the table, munching on some dry-roasted, Morgan glanced at the bar but Nicola had disappeared. He sulked while Kiddie sat down and carried on with his monologue. He was barely listening as he heard the life story of one Frankie Bosser, a local Woodvale lad turned successful villain. Or villain of sorts. Morgan knew importing drink in big quantities wasn't legal, but a lot of people did it. There were far worse crimes around.

'And then a few years ago it all went wrong,' Kiddie concluded ten minutes later. 'Frankie had to do a runner when he shot a policeman who was snooping in the grounds of his house one night. Frankie was the next one up for the customs investigators, and this policeman was trying to earn a few brownie points by doing some work on his own. He was a constable called Cady. We had been at Hendon together so I knew him vaguely: nice guy but not too bright. Had to be spoon-fed at Hendon to make it through. Was still a constable after all this time. So when Frankie made his getaway, he was driven to the coast by the recently deceased Stanley Bosser. He caught a hovercraft into France and disappeared. We've heard nothing of him since.'

'And now he's coming back for the funeral and you want to catch him?'

'That's the general idea.'

'Are the airports looking out for him?'

'Yeah. But I suspect he's back already.'

'So we keep an eye on his mother's house and check all the local hotels.'

'Stepmother, actually. She's Italian, as I said.'

'So that's probably where he's been hiding.'

'Where?'

'Italy.'

Kiddie nodded. 'Could be.'

Morgan finished his beer. 'I'll ask Cole if we can spare a man on every shift to keep an eye on the Bosser house. Bosser will have to go there sooner or later. When he does, we'll pick him up.'

'OK. I wouldn't mind doing it myself. I'm not exactly up to my oxters.'

Morgan laughed. Kiddie liked dropping the odd Scottish word into conversations to baffle everyone. Loosely translated, oxters means armpits.

'And what about the person who punched out Stanley Bosser?' Morgan asked.

'Well, he's vanished without trace. We got some good descriptions of him and we're keeping a look out, interviewing the usual suspects.'

'OK. That's about all you can do. Probably won't get him though. And now I have to get back to the exciting world of paperwork.'

'I'll come with you.'

'No, you go on ahead,' Morgan said. 'I just want a word with Nicola.'

Kiddie gave him a knowing look and walked out of the pub. Morgan picked up the glasses and walked over to the bar.

That same Thursday lunchtime, Phil Gator decided it was time he got off his backside and found himself a job. He needed to get some money rolling in.

He had spent the past couple of days getting up late, watching *Home and Away* on TV (the actresses were better looking than on *Neighbours*), then getting restless in the afternoons. He listened to the news on the local radio stations to see if there was anything about him punching the old bloke, but nothing was mentioned. Far too insignificant, he supposed.

When his mother returned in the evenings from the swimming pool, they would have supper together and catch up on old news. She would cook him something basic like frozen hamburgers with potatoes and peas, or fishfingers and chips. Then she would lend him five pounds so he could go to the pub up the road and have two pints, and leave her in peace to watch TV.

In the pub Gator kept the regulars entertained with his exploits in Europe, but he was already bored with that routine. He managed to scrounge a few extra pints, but what he really needed was to get laid.

On the third evening, last night, he had wandered around from pub to pub until he had stumbled upon one of his old flames, a lovely looking girl called Wendy with long, dark, frizzy hair. Wendy was not too bright and easy to manipulate, and he had persuaded her to give him a hand-job in the car park outside the pub. He was pretty certain that if he'd had his own place he would've been able to persuade her to go back with him: a good reason why he should start looking for work. Still, the hand-job had been good, leaning up against the outside wall of the men's lavatory.

Although he had been boasting about his sex life in Europe to the regulars in the pub, the truth was quite different, and he had only managed one quick screw in his whole three months away.

That had been on a campsite in the South of France, when an overweight Australian girl who had been eyeing him all day on the beach came into his tent, unzipped his sleeping-bag and sat right down on top of him. He'd hardly had any choice in the matter, and when she'd left him ten minutes later Gator had logged it in his memory as the worst screw he'd ever had. But now back home in England that quick encounter was beginning to look like the fuck of the century.

Maybe he could get a bit further with Wendy tonight, he thought, but he knew she didn't trust him at all. Their affair about a year ago lasted four months, and, unknown to Wendy, Gator had been seeing other women on the side. Maybe she had found out about that while he'd been away.

There were no mechanic's jobs in the local paper, so Gator applied for a job as a fork-lift driver on the outskirts of Redgate, which was only three or four miles from his mother's house. He rang the number, found the job was still available and had a quick shower. He put on a clean pair of jeans and a white T-shirt, and walked out of the front door.

He caught a bus in Woodvale High Street, and got off in Redgate before the bus started going around the one-way system in the wrong direction. Then he had a ten-minute stroll in the sun to the Holmethorpe Industrial Estate which was next to the railway line that took commuters into London. He walked under the railway bridge and looked at the signpost at the entrance to the estate, which gave the locations of all the different companies. There were about thirty businesses listed there, including car showrooms, a plastics factory, a tool factory, and even one that made thermometers. Gator was looking for Ellis Pipes, and followed the road that led to the left.

Ellis Pipes was another five-minute walk away, down a rutted track over wasteland, then past a British Industrial Sand factory, some warehouses and a canteen. Gator passed workers wearing yellow hardhats, and dodged a lorry that drove right at him. Then he came to a builders' yard to the side of the factory, without any sign, which he presumed was Ellis Pipes. He headed towards a Portakabin, knocked on the door and walked in.

The first person he saw was an old guy sitting behind a desk.

'I've come about the fork-lift job,' Gator said. 'I rang up earlier.'

'Oh yes,' said the old guy. He looked about ninety to Gator. Why was he still working? 'Brian will interview you.'

Gator turned to his left, and a big bloke stood up, with short, dark hair and a moustache. He held out his hand and introduced himself as the foreman. 'Let's go outside,' he said.

They stepped out of the office and into the builders' yard.

'You've driven a fork-lift before, have you?' Brian asked.

Gator nodded and reached in his pocket. 'I've got a fork-lift licence,' he said. 'It's from a few years ago, but I still remember how to drive one.'

He handed over the piece of paper and watched Brian as he studied it. Gator had never passed a fork-lift test at all. He had photocopied the form from one of his friends who'd worked in a factory, then Tipp-exed out his friend's name and put in his own. Gator knew how to drive a fork-lift, though, from a factory job he'd had in the past. They were not difficult to handle, and being a mechanic he knew how to drive most vehicles.

'This is a photocopy,' Brian said.

'I lost my original,' Gator said. 'I had to ring up the factory and ask for a replacement.'

Brian nodded. 'Fair enough. But before I explain anything about the job, I'd better see you drive.'

'OK,' Gator said. 'Lead the way. That one over there?'

There was an orange fork-lift a few yards away. Gator jumped in, checked the gear was in neutral and turned it on. He listened as Brian shouted out what he wanted him to do. He put the machine into gear, and trundled over to a pack of brown pipes on a pallet. He eased the two forks under the pallet, lifted them

43

up in one steady movement, and reversed. Then he drove round to another stack and put the pallet gently on top. He eased the forks out, reversed nicely and parked.

Brian waved him over to another stack and Gator did the same again. He parked the fork-lift and grinned at Brian from his seat. 'Anything else?' he asked.

Brian wandered over. 'That's OK,' he said. 'Just turn it off and I'll show you round.'

They walked around the builders' yard, which was about the size of a football pitch. There were different stacks of pipes and fittings, lots of odd shapes and sizes. A wire-mesh fence went all round the perimeter. Rough, unused land surrounded the yard, and along one side was a dip into a valley before the ground rose again in the distance. On the top of the far hill was the skeleton of the now shut-down Fuller's Earth factory.

'All we do here', Brian said, 'is stack up lorries when they come in, and unstack deliveries. We're not too busy at the moment because we've only been open a few months. So there's a lot of hanging around.'

'And where do I hang around?' asked Gator.

'There's a storeroom by the entrance. Just before you get to the office. That'll be your home. It'll just be a case of sitting in there until a lorry turns up. There'll be other yard work as well, though. Mr Carroll sees to that.'

'Mr Carroll's the old guy?'

'Yeah. He's from up north. That's where our head office is. They sent him down to get this yard open and keep him busy. He'll leave eventually and let me run things.'

'He looks too old to be working.'

'You're right. He's seventy-five. He lives alone, though, and doesn't have anything better to do.'

'Is he all right to work for?'

'He's fine,' Brian said, but he didn't sound too convincing to Gator.

'What's the pay like?' he asked.

'We pay five pounds an hour for a forty-hour week. That's two hundred a week. We can pay you weekly or monthly, it's up to you.'

Gator nearly fell over. He could earn a lot more as a mechanic, but it would have to do for now. He asked to be paid weekly, and Brian led him back to the office to fill in some forms.

'Do you lift weights?' Brian asked as they walked.

Gator looked at him. 'No. Why?'

'You've got big arms. I thought you might work out. I do a bit myself.'

'I'm a mechanic by trade,' Gator said. 'You get strong arms wrestling under a car all day.'

Brian nodded. Gator would have to watch this bloke. He was still looking at his arms. Was he a queer or something?

When they got back to the office Mr Carroll introduced himself and Gator knew this was one old fart he'd never get on with. The guy was like something from *The Bridge on the River Kwai*, an old-generation army colonel who should be sitting on a porch somewhere in the Far East sipping a gin and tonic. In a separate room behind Carroll was another man, a friendly, smiling, middle-aged chap called Ridley, who came out and shook Gator's hand. Ridley was wearing a bow tie.

After completing some forms Gator was soon out of there, walking away with a spring in his step. They had told him to start on Monday. That left him tomorrow and the weekend to live it up. He could borrow some extra money off his mother now that he had a job, and take Wendy out for a meal or something. Maybe they could progress a little from the handjob in the car park, to the bedroom at her parents' house.

6

At about midday on Friday Jason Campbell was down in his basement playing guitar when he heard a car engine outside. He stopped mid-song, went to the back door and walked up the stone steps into the garden. Turning right into the drive, he saw Karl climbing out of a blue car.

'Jason, my man,' said Karl, smiling. 'Here comes the first of the fleet.' He walked over with his hand outstretched and Jason shook it.

'I thought you were moving in tomorrow,' Jason said.

'Well, I had nothing much to do today, so I thought I may as well make a start. It doesn't muck you up, does it?'

'Not really. It's just that I've got a lesson in about an hour. I'm just preparing for that now.'

'Well, you go on preparing. Don't worry about me.'

Jason nodded. 'I'd better move my Mini out before you start bringing cars in. I need it this evening.'

'No problemo. I'll move this right now.'

Jason winced at the no problemo. Did people still speak like that? He'd probably be saying okey-dokey next. He went back inside the house to get his car keys, then came out and moved his Mini on to the street. He watched as Karl drove the blue car, a Nissan, into the garage. He couldn't help but feel a tinge of regret at his loss of freedom, and reminded himself to think of his healthy bank balance instead.

Back in the basement, Jason tried to concentrate on the forthcoming lesson. He was going to teach a new finger-picking style to one of his best students, and it was a technique he hardly used himself. He sat and went over it again and again, and by the time the front doorbell rang he reckoned he had it pretty much worked out.

He walked up the basement stairs that led into the hall and opened the front door. His student was a tall, gangly twenty-year-old called Barry. He had long straight dark hair and hunched shoulders. He reminded Jason of a youthful Neil Young. When he'd let Barry in Jason looked to see if there was any sign of Karl, but the coast was clear.

They went down to the basement, sat opposite each other, and started practising. Ten minutes later though, the sound of another car came from the drive outside. Barry gave Jason a quizzical look.

'It's my new lodger,' Jason said. 'I've had to take one to get some money coming in.' He tried to laugh it off. 'You'd better learn right now that you'll never make any money as a musician.'

They continued practising and Jason thought all was quiet on the driveway front, until he heard Karl start to sing. It was one of those loud, over-the-top voices, by someone who thinks he can sing but can't. And what was worse was the song. Karl was singing 'Wake Me Up Before You Go-Go' by Wham, one of the corniest pop songs in history as far as Jason was concerned. He started seething inside and tried to concentrate on his playing. Karl's singing kept coming through, though, and a few minutes later Jason had to stop.

'I'll be back in a minute,' he said to Barry. 'I'll see if I can shut Pavarotti up.'

Jason walked out of the basement door and on to the drive. Karl was carrying a cardboard box into the garage where the Nissan was parked. In the drive now was a red Fiat. Karl stopped mid-song when he saw Jason, who gave him a stiff smile.

'You couldn't stop singing, could you, Karl? I'm trying to teach someone downstairs and your voice is coming right through. Much as I like Wham.'

47

'No problemo, my man,' Karl said. 'I didn't know you were down there. You should've told me.'

'I did tell you, actually. I didn't know you'd be back so soon. I'll have to give you a list of when I'm teaching every week.'

'That's a good idea.'

'I'll see you later,' Jason said, turning back towards the basement.

'Can you play any Wham songs?' Karl asked, as Jason was about to disappear.

Jason turned and looked at Karl, this tough-looking guy with the shaved head and the goatee, standing there holding a cardboard box full of junk as if it had no weight at all. This tough-looking guy who was obviously a Wham fan.

'I've never tried,' Jason said. 'But I'll see what I can do.' Then he went back into the basement.

Karl carried his cardboard box into the garage and put it on a workbench at the back. Then he walked out to the Fiat and started carrying bits of his stereo into the house. He was in a good mood.

He liked this new home of his, this three-bedroomed, semi-detached, solid-looking house. He preferred this older style. His last lodgings had been on a new estate in Redgate, and Nick, the bloke he shared with, had worked for Pizza Hut as a personnel manager. Karl found that quite ironic. Deal with people's problems all day at work and then come home and treat Karl like shit. Karl would get his own back on Nick one day, though, and that Spanish girlfriend of his, Theresa, who had taken his place. He would think of some sly way of paying them back for the inconvenience. And it was a pity because business had been going so well. Now he would have to let people know his new address and get things rolling again.

Karl had been interested in cars for as long as he could remember. As a child he had first become smitten when watching Formula One on TV. Like most small boys he had wanted to become a racing driver – James Hunt had been his favourite – but this dream had soon vanished when the practicalities of adult life had reared their heads.

At the age of eighteen he had bought his first car, a Ford Escort, done a little work on it, and sold it for a hundred pounds' profit a few months later. The rest of his working life had proceeded in exactly the same manner. Nowadays he scoured car magazines and local papers, bought cars that were a little under-priced, got a friend of his to carry out any mechanical work that might need doing, and then sold them for a healthy profit. He only needed to sell four or five cars a month to be able to make a comfortable living. After all, he wasn't paying any tax. What the fuck was that all about, anyway?

Karl carried the amp and tape deck into his room and put them on the floor by the window. Then he went down for the rest of his stereo.

He spent the next half-hour plugging in leads and positioning the speakers. He really wanted to blast some music out, but thought he'd better wait until Jason's lesson had finished. Jason seemed an OK bloke to him, a bit of a square dude, but there were plenty of those around. After all, Nick from Pizza Hut hadn't exactly been Mr Hip. Karl thought that in a way it was better to live with someone a bit straight, so that his own rough edges wouldn't be so obvious to the neighbours. And straight people were easier to manipulate and usually didn't have the guts to stand up to him. Except for that bastard Nick, of course. Well, he'd get his one day.

After setting up the stereo, Karl brought in some clothes and laid them in the chest of drawers. He owned mostly jeans and T-shirts, with a few smart things in case he fancied a night in a local disco. He wasn't that interested in clothes. Then he walked back on to the landing and headed down the stairs.

He heard voices below and found Jason and a long-haired grunge-type talking in the hall. Jason introduced him and Karl shook the wimpy-looking guy's hand. The wimpy-looking guy gave him a strange look then walked out of the door carrying his guitar.

Karl turned to Jason and said, 'I thought the sixties ended a few decades ago.'

Jason smiled and said, 'Just leaving, were you?' And then walked off to the kitchen.

Karl didn't like the sarcastic tone in Jason's voice, even though it had been accompanied by a smile. Karl would have to keep an eye on him. He didn't want his new landlord getting out of line.

Driving a rented Ford Sierra on the same Friday afternoon, Frankie Bosser was now a man on a mission. What had started out as a straightforward trip over to England for his father's funeral was now getting a lot more complicated.

When he telephoned Daniela on Tuesday and tried to arrange a meeting, she said it was out of the question. She suspected that the police would soon be watching her house. Frankie had asked why, and Daniela told him how his father had been punched by a hooligan. She hadn't mentioned this when she'd rung him in Italy. Frankie held his head in his hands, feeling a burning rage in his chest. He asked her for details and she said to wait until they met.

On the Wednesday Frankie had gone out in the morning and rented the Sierra, then driven into the country to a secluded pub in some woods near South Godstone. He arrived thirty minutes late, because the pub was so secluded he was unable to find the damn thing. There in the restaurant he ate lunch with Daniela, who had sneaked out of the back of her house, and caught a taxi to the pub. She told him all she knew about his father's attack, about the Railway pub, about how Stanley didn't know why he'd been punched. Then she described the heart attack in the bath. She also said that because of the coroner's inquiry the funeral wouldn't be able to take place for a while. Frankie asked how long that would be and Daniela said, 'How long is a piece of string?'

Frankie swore out loud. Maybe he should've stayed in Italy until the complications had been cleared.

After catching up on old times, Frankie drove Daniela back to Redgate for the short taxi ride back to her house. From now on they would speak only on the telephone.

So while he was waiting for the funeral to take place, Frankie was going to try to find out who punched his father. A good place to start was the Railway pub. He parked in the large car park and walked into the almost empty saloon bar. He ordered an orange juice from the barman and lit up a cigarette. There was a TV above the bar with a tennis match on it, the sound turned down very low. Frankie had heard how nearly every bar in England now had a TV showing satellite sport, and how in winter the bars became packed when football was on. Frankie found it incredibly depressing to think how most of the male population's interest seemed to end at football and beer. What kind of a life was that? It seemed he had left the country at the right time.

When the barman had finished giving him his change Frankie said, 'I hear you had some trouble here earlier this week. Out in the car park?'

The barman looked at him suspiciously. 'What kind of trouble?'

Frankie took a sip of his orange. 'Some old man collapsed in the car park after getting punched by a young guy.'

The barman nodded. 'That was my day off. I heard about it. Are you a policeman?'

Frankie laughed. 'No. I'm the old man's lawyer. I told him to press charges so I'm trying to find the young guy that did it.'

The barman gave Frankie the once over. Frankie had dressed in a suit and tie for this encounter – playing the part of a lawyer – and reckoned he looked pretty convincing, although possibly not as smooth as a lawyer. But at least he appeared official; more like a cop really, so the barman had made a decent guess.

The barman pointed behind Frankie. 'You see that old boy

over there? Go and talk to him. He practically lives here. His name's Joe.'

Frankie thanked him and took his glass over to where Joe was sitting. 'Afternoon,' he said. 'Mind if I join you?'

Joe looked up from his newspaper with surprise, then looked around the pub to make sure Frankie was talking to him. Frankie found that quite amusing considering there were only about five other people in the bar.

'Join me for what?' Joe asked.

'The barman said you're a regular here. I need to ask you some questions.'

Joe folded his newspaper and motioned with his hand. 'Feel free,' he said.

Frankie sat down and gave him the lawyer story he'd just given the barman. Joe looked about seventy-five to Frankie, a tanned face, bald over most of his head, except for some longish pure-white hair at the sides. He was wearing a light blue shirt unbuttoned about halfway down his chest that revealed a tanned V round his neck, and white chest hairs lower down. He had a deep, rough-sounding voice and looked like a manual worker to Frankie, rough hands to go with the voice.

'That was Monday, I think,' Joe said. 'Monday afternoon.'

'About four o'clock?'

'That's right. I was sitting here, of course. Never sit anywhere else. I'd just gone to the bar to get a drink, and when I looked out of the door I saw the whole thing.'

He had Frankie's complete attention. 'You saw the whole thing,' he said. 'Can you tell me what happened?'

Joe took a sip of his pint, little more than a wetting of the lips. At that rate it probably took him an hour to finish a whole pint. He rested the glass back softly on the table and turned to face the door Frankie had just walked through. 'I was coming from the bar, and passing the door over there. I saw the old guy's van parked outside, and then this young long-haired bloke comes over to the van and pulls him out.'

'What did the young bloke look like?' Frankie waited as Joe searched through his memory.

'He had long blond hair, nearly to his shoulders. Straight hair. And he was unshaven. Looked a real mess.'

'A hippy type?'

'Yeah, but he wasn't built like no hippy. I thought it was a bit odd. He was strong looking, had a physique on him. You don't see body-builder types with long hair and beards.'

Frankie nodded. He had to agree with that. 'Did he pull him out of the van straight away, or say something first?'

Joe said, 'Let's go outside. I might remember better if I'm out there.'

They left their drinks and Joe's newspaper on the table and ambled outside. Joe was as tall as Frankie, but had a creaky gait resulting from aching muscles and ageing bones. They walked to the side of the car park and Joe started talking again.

'The van was parked here,' he said, making motions with his hands. 'Now the young bloke came up and opened the driver's door straight away. The driver was sitting inside having a smoke. The young bloke said something, pulled the driver out and pushed him up against the side of the van.'

Joe was acting it all out as he spoke. Frankie was thinking this guy must watch a lot of TV. He knew all the right moves. It was like seeing a stuntman rehearsing a fight scene.

'He smashed the driver with a right-hander to the chin, then a left-hander to the stomach. As he was falling, he kneed him in the face. The driver was out cold on the tarmac.' Joe stood back a pace as if a body had just fallen in front of him.

Frankie found it painful to listen to such a precise account of his father's beating, but at least it gave him a fuller picture, while also fuelling his anger. 'What happened then?' he asked.

Joe looked at Frankie for the first time since he'd started his fight routine and said, 'He just walked away. Down the street.'

'Which way?'

'To the left. I'd walked outside by then. If I'd been younger I would've run after him. But you don't stand a chance when you get to my age.'

Frankie looked off down the street. 'Did anyone else see all this?'

'Yeah,' said Joe. 'A few people were watching from the road. A crowd gathered round the driver as well.'

'Was he unconscious for long?'

'No. Someone poured a glass of water over his face and that woke him up. We told him the police were on their way, but he just got into his van and drove off. Said he didn't want to talk to the police.'

Frankie knew the reason for that. 'Is there anything else you can remember about the young man? Did you think he was a local? I suppose he must've been if he just walked off.'

Joe had to think about that. Frankie waited patiently then saw a light come on behind the old man's eyes.

'There is one thing,' he said. 'He had a rucksack. He picked up a rucksack from the ground and slung it over his shoulder. That must've been why he was all unshaven and long-haired. He must've been travelling a while.'

There were a few butterflies stirring in Frankie's stomach. Now they were getting somewhere. 'But was he a down and out? A homeless person?'

'No.' Joe shook his head. 'He was too healthy looking, too strong. He must've just come back from abroad. Maybe hitching somewhere or something. Did a bit of it myself when I was younger. He had walking boots on as well. Walking boots, jeans, greenish anorak, white T-shirt. And carrying that rucksack. It's amazing what you can remember when you want to.'

Frankie patted him on the arm. 'You've been a great help, Joe,' he said. He reached into his pocket and brought out a ten-pound note. 'Buy yourself a drink. Buy yourself two!'

Joe reached out and took the money. 'That's the first time a lawyer's given me money.' He chuckled. 'I'll take it.'

Frankie laughed, shook Joe's hand and walked back to his car.

As he sat behind the wheel he tried to think of what to do next. He knew more about his father's killer than he had fifteen minutes ago, but where the hell would he look next? He decided to drive around a bit, and see if any inspiration hit him. He started the engine and turned left out of the car park.

7

That same Friday, before leaving work at six, Detective Inspector Jesse Morgan rang up the Police National Computer at Hendon to see if they had any information on Frankie Bosser. The man on the other end of the phone told him Bosser was listed there as a wanted man, but nothing much else was known about him. He mentioned the importing of booze from France, how Bosser was next in line for an investigation about that, and a little about Constable Cady, the policeman Bosser had shot. Bosser was now forty-one. He was six foot. He had short blond hair. Morgan left his office and went home.

On the short drive to his rented house Morgan had more important things than Frankie Bosser on his mind. Tonight he was taking Nicola from the Red Lion out for a meal, and for the first time in quite a while he felt a bit of adrenaline running through his normally unexcited body. He'd asked her out yesterday lunchtime after getting rid of Kiddie, and to his great surprise she had agreed without hesitation. Morgan's record with women had not been too good recently, and anything that happened these days was something of a shock and a bonus. Maybe his luck was about to change.

Five minutes later he was driving his unmarked car on to the parking area of the housing estate where he lived. There was a row of garages there but he seldom used the one allocated to him. He was always popping in and out, and life was too short to be opening and closing garage doors all the time.

Morgan rented a three-bedroomed semi-detached which was about ten years old, and looked exactly like all the other houses on the estate. He unlocked the front door, and dropped his keys on the hall table. He picked up the mail off the floor, saw there was nothing of interest, so dropped it all in the waste bin that he kept by the front door for that specific purpose. Then he walked up the narrow stairs to his bedroom.

To describe the house as three-bedroomed was undeserved flattery. There was one large bedroom looking out over the front, and two small shoeboxes. Morgan always thought of it as a one-bedroomed house with two half-attempts.

He walked into the first small room at the top of the stairs and started undressing. In here there was just a low double bed and a wardrobe, nothing on the walls, and no bedside table. Morgan only entered it to change or sleep so he didn't care about the decor. He used the large bedroom as a second sitting room and reading room, and the other small bedroom for dumping junk. He hung his suit up in the wardrobe, chucked everything else into a laundry basket, and walked into the bathroom next door.

He stood under the shower for five minutes, and shampooed his short dark hair and beard. He had only had the beard for a year or so, giving up on the previous moustache after just about everyone he met kept saying he looked like the American actor Dennis Weaver. He was not a big fan of Weaver or that hick cop character McCloud he used to play on TV. Now when he looked in the mirror Morgan thought he looked a little like the country singer and actor Kris Kristofferson, but not many people knew who Kristofferson was so he was satisfied with this new appearance. The beard also made him look more distinguished and worldly-wise, and that was an image he could live with. Even though he felt about as worldly-wise as he had at the age of twenty.

Stepping from the shower, Morgan dried his lean body, blow-dried his hair and beard, and went back to the bedroom. Staring into the wardrobe, he wondered what he should wear from the basic selection that he possessed. He wanted something smart and yet not too formal. He hated looking like an off-duty cop. He settled on black jeans, cream-coloured shirt, and a light brown sports jacket. On his feet he wore suede loafers.

Pleased with this look, he walked downstairs into the living room. He turned on the stereo and put on a CD by a new country singer called John Berry, then went into the kitchen which looked out on a neat back garden laid to lawn, with a few small bushes here and there that Morgan hardly needed to touch. Feeling the need for some Dutch courage, he opened his drinks cabinet and mixed himself a whisky and American. He sat at the kitchen table and stared into the garden, while Berry sang a romantic ballad in the background. Morgan had always been a country-music fan, ever since his teens, and it amused him to think how it had now become fashionable, after all these years, when before he had been regarded by his friends as a square for liking such hillbilly rubbish. What goes around comes around, he thought, as he finished off the drink.

He was about to turn off the CD when Berry started singing an old Bruce Springsteen song called 'Thunder Road'. Morgan preferred the Springsteen version, but this one was a good enough attempt. He stood in the middle of the lounge thinking back to a Springsteen concert he'd been to years ago in Brighton before Bruce had become really famous. That had been one of the highlights of his life, a night of loud, rocking music, and dancing in the aisles. Morgan had been jumping with the crowd, barely ten feet away from Springsteen at the front of the stage. The concert had left him high for about two weeks and life had suddenly seemed full of possibilities. Then a few months later Morgan had joined the police force. If Bruce could see him now, he thought, what would he think?

He turned off the CD when the song had finished, picked up his car keys, and walked out of the front door. He was meeting Nicola in a pub in Woodvale and wanted to get there before she did. He didn't want her to be waiting on her own, and it would give him an excuse to have another drink. Before he did that, though, he needed to drop his car at the police station and cadge a lift off someone to the pub. He intended to have a few drinks tonight, and it wouldn't do to be driving as well.

He was sitting at the bar in the Bell, most of the way through a pint of Murphy's, when Nicola walked in. Morgan watched her coming towards him with a smile on her face. She was wearing blue jeans, brown boots and a black blouse. She was about five-eight, and had slim, slightly bowed legs. Her short dark hair looked freshly washed, and she had no make-up on. She looked a bit like Sandra Bullock to Morgan, the actress in *Speed*. He smiled at the thought. Sandra and Kris on their first date together.

He got off his stool as she got nearer and said hello.

Nicola said, 'Finish your drink and come with me. I've changed my mind about eating out.'

Morgan reached for his Murphy's. 'You mean you're cancelling our date?'

Nicola shook her head. 'No. I'm taking you back to my place. I've fixed us a meal. We can buy some wine on the way.'

Morgan liked the idea of that, and knocked back his drink in one. 'Let's go,' he said.

Nicola hung on to his arm as they walked up Woodvale High Street. It was a warm summer's evening and would be another hour or so before nightfall. Morgan thought it was the kind of evening when it was great to be alive, living in England, and walking with a pretty woman on your arm. His earlier melancholy drifted away.

'How come your name is Jesse?' Nicola asked. 'That's an unusual Christian name.'

Morgan chuckled. He'd been asked that many times. He was surprised Nicola hadn't asked him before, but, then again, they'd never really talked that much in the Red Lion. 'It was my father's choice,' he said. 'He was a big fan of Westerns. He wanted his son to be a cowboy but obviously that wasn't going to happen in

England. So he gave me a cowboy name instead. It seems like he wasn't too far off the mark anyway. I've turned out to be some kind of sheriff.'

'You look like a cowboy too,' Nicola teased. 'With that beard. I can imagine you walking into a saloon for a whisky and a shoot-out.'

'Not much chance of a shoot-out in Woodvale.'

'You're telling me. When does the excitement begin around here?'

They stopped at an off-licence, and bought two bottles of Italian white. Then it was just a little further to Nicola's flat. She unlocked a door between two shops, and led him up an undecorated staircase to the flats above. They walked down a straight, linoleum-floored corridor which was dimly lit. Nicola noticed Morgan's worried look and said, 'Don't worry, the flats are all right.'

She unlocked the door to flat number six and led him in. He hung up his jacket in the corridor and followed her into a large room. It was a studio flat and on the left was a double bed. The far side was all windows, and next to them were a small sofa and armchair, a TV and hi-fi unit. Morgan walked over and looked out of the window. There was a residents' car park below, and then over some trees he could see Woodvale Priory. He went jogging there sometimes. It had a couple of duck ponds, football pitches and rolling hills, only they weren't rolling when you were trying to run up them.

'Nice view,' he said. 'Is this your own flat?'

Nicola was standing next to him. 'I bought it six months ago. I had to sell our house when David died, and bought this instead.'

Morgan looked at her with shock. 'You're getting ahead of me,' he said. 'Was David your husband?'

Nicola nodded. 'I thought you knew.'

'Why would I?' Morgan said. 'We've only small-talked in the pub.'

'I thought everyone there knew. They're always giving me sympathetic looks like I'll never get over it. I probably never will, but I could do without the sympathy all the time.'

'How long ago was this?'

'A year and a half. Liver cancer. From diagnosis to death was six months. It was a terrible time.' Nicola laughed bitterly. 'That must be the biggest understatement of the year.'

'That's bad. I'm sorry. I didn't know.' Morgan could think of nothing else to say.

'Let's get a drink,' Nicola said.

They went into the small kitchen at the side, where places had already been set on a Formica kitchen table. Nicola reached in a drawer and pulled out a corkscrew.

'Here,' she said, handing it to him. 'Men do it much better.'

Morgan busied himself with the two bottles while Nicola got out some large glasses and put two cubes of ice in each. He poured the wine into them, big generous helpings, then put the bottles into the fridge. He held his glass up to hers and said, 'Cheers.' They chinked them together.

The meal Nicola had prepared was a salad, with a selection of ham and cheeses and French bread. They talked about Morgan's police career, a brief rundown of the last twenty years. He had joined at the age of twenty-six, in the Met to start with, then the River Police, then slowly moved out of the city into the suburbs. He had been in Borough Heath in south London for about five years, before moving further south into this slow-moving, respectable area of Surrey.

'I thought I'd prefer it out here,' he said, 'in the so-called country, but it's so boring I'm thinking of giving it up altogether.'

'Couldn't you just quit and get a good pension?'

'I could, but what else would I do? Become a security guard and get fat and lazy?'

'You could open a pub and I could come and help you.' Nicola took another sip of wine and laughed. They were on the second bottle now, the salad all gone, the French bread lying in pieces on their side plates.

'If I worked in a pub, I'd become an alcoholic,' Morgan said. 'I already drink too much. How long have you been at the Red Lion?'

'Only since David died. When I sold the house I had quite a bit left over, so I didn't need a full-time job. Plus David was heavily insured, bless him. Sometimes I think that maybe I should get back into full-time work to take my mind off things, but then I think what's the point? Work isn't that important. I prefer just to make a bit of money and see my friends the rest of the time. Or go into London if I need a bit of excitement. I like going to concerts.'

'What sort of concerts?'

'I like rock concerts or country music, things like that.'

Morgan nearly dropped his glass of wine. 'You like country music?' he asked with surprise. 'Same as me. Who do you like?'

'Come and see my record collection.'

They walked through into the main room with their wineglasses and sat on the floor in front of the stereo. They spent the next few hours listening to music and going through Nicola's CD collection. She put on Nanci Griffith and Morgan fell immediately in love with her voice. Then Nicola played some Rosanne Cash, and Iris DeMent, two more great singers. Finally they put on Lyle Lovett.

'You know the first time I heard Lyle Lovett?' Morgan said to Nicola. The wine had all gone now and she was sipping a Baileys, while Morgan had a Bell's. 'I was working in Borough Heath about four years ago. This guy got mugged there one evening and started trying to find out who mugged him, to get some sort of revenge. The whole thing ended up in a terrible mess. Well, I went round to see this guy in the local YMCA where he was living. When I got to his room he had Lyle Lovett playing on his cassette player. I bought one of the albums a few days later. I liked it a lot, thought it was intelligent, witty country music. Then, much to my surprise, this young guy at the YMCA got involved in a manslaughter charge and nearly ruined his life completely in the space of a few days. I couldn't figure out why. I thought, if someone is intelligent enough to listen to Lyle Lovett, why would they want to get mixed up in crime?'

'So you're saying that all criminals have bad taste in music?'

'I'm saying all criminals probably don't listen to serious music. All music generates emotion and country music certainly doesn't make you feel aggressive. The opposite, I would've thought.'

'I think that's a big generalization. I'm sure even murderers listen to serious music,' Nicola said.

'Maybe. But I still felt disappointed. I can honestly say he was the first person I've arrested who liked country music. To the best of my knowledge, of course. I obviously don't know the musical taste of everyone I've locked up.'

'That could be an interesting survey. Maybe there's a common link between what criminals listen to. Maybe certain beats or rhythms lead them to crime.'

'Maybe I could introduce it into my interviews. "Now what's your favourite kind of music?" That would throw them.'

Nicola laughed. 'I think maybe you've had too much to drink.'

Morgan nodded. 'And I have to work tomorrow.'

'Early shift?'

Morgan nodded. 'Six to two. Then a week of two to ten then a week of ten to six. With days off in between, of course. But if something serious happens, you have to work all hours. Although nothing very serious has happened since I've been here.'

Lyle Lovett's 'Closing Time' came on the stereo. They sat and listened to the lyrics: about shutting up a bar and getting rid of the customers after a night of music and drinking. It seemed an appropriate song to end on.

'I think he's trying to tell us something,' Morgan said when it had finished.

Nicola looked at the clock on the stereo. 'Twelve-thirty. He could be right.'

There was an uncomfortable silence, the first of the evening, then Morgan climbed slowly to his feet and stretched.

'Can I use your phone?' he asked. 'I need a cab.'

While they waited for the cab they talked some more about country music. Morgan smiled at her. He felt something stirring deep inside, a feeling he hadn't experienced for a long time. He wished he could stay longer but his policeman's training came first, always holding him back when maybe sometimes he should just let go. He knew there would be other times, though. This was certainly going to lead somewhere, he was as sure about that as he had been about anything in the past few years.

The doorbell rang and startled him. He got to his feet.

'So what happened to the Lyle Lovett fan?' Nicola asked as they walked to the front door. 'Did he go to gaol?'

Morgan shook his head. 'No. He got a suspended sentence.'

'So he's probably still listening to the same records.'

'Probably. And I hope he's learned from his mistakes.'

Morgan thanked her for the evening and kissed her on the cheek. He thought she looked a little disappointed.

And then he was walking down the corridor. He would wait until he was out of sight, on the staircase going down, before he started punching the air.

8

Jason Campbell spent most of Saturday wondering if he had made a big mistake. He was down in the basement practising on his keyboards, trying to write the middle-eight of a new song, and making every effort to keep out of Karl's way as he moved in yet more cars and belongings. Jason's Mini was now parked on the street outside, and it looked as though it would be there permanently, while Karl used the whole drive and the garage.

Karl had disappeared for the rest of Friday after the first two cars had arrived, and Jason's second lesson of the day had taken place in peace. But today Karl was back with the third car, more singing in the drive, then a lift back to Redgate with a friend for the fourth car. Karl had also asked if he could invite a few friends round in the evening for a house-warming party. Jason had asked how many friends, and Karl had replied four or five. Jason had reluctantly agreed.

Now Jason was starting to get worried.

He stopped playing, walked up the stairs and entered the living room. As Karl would no doubt have everyone in here, he looked around to see if there was anything breakable or nickable. He decided he'd better take his hi-fi to his bedroom along with all the CDs and cassettes.

Karl was driving a cream Azura now, and he pulled it into the drive on Naughton Road. He parked it snugly behind the red Fiat and carried another box of belongings to the front door. He unlocked the door, holding the box with one arm. As he stepped into the hall, Jason was coming out of the living room with a stack of CDs.

'Hey, Jason,' he said. 'What're you up to?'

'Just clearing out the living room for your party,' Jason said. 'So you've got room for your guests.'

Karl looked at the CDs Jason was holding.

'Don't you trust us then? Think some of those might go missing?'

'You never know,' Jason said. 'It's better not to take the risk.'

Then he was walking past Karl going up the stairs with his haul. Karl followed him up and looked at Jason's bare legs. He was wearing green shorts today, with a blue shirt tucked inside them, brown leather shoes with grey socks.

'Nice legs, Jason,' he joked, and Jason laughed over his shoulder. Well, that was an improvement, Karl thought.

When they reached the upstairs landing Karl asked, 'Are you taking your stereo out too?'

'I thought I would,' Jason said. 'I'll probably just listen to music in my room from now on.'

Karl looked into the small bedroom which was going to be Jason's hiding place. There were posters of rock singers on the walls whom Karl didn't recognize, a single bed and two chests of drawers. Instead of a window there were double doors leading on to a small balcony.

'I didn't know you had a balcony,' Karl said.

'I intend to sit out there as the sun goes down,' Jason replied, 'sipping on a glass of wine.'

Karl was starting to feel jealous.

'You don't want to swap rooms do you?' Jason asked.

'No way.' Karl shook his head. 'I need to spread out a bit. I'll leave you to it.'

He went into his bedroom and placed the latest box on the carpet. He then had to dodge round other boxes to reach the stereo on the floor. He started unplugging and untangling cables, which was a bit annoying after plugging it all in yesterday. Still, if

66

Jason wanted to be petty and hide all his things away, it meant that Karl could move his stuff into the living room, and, in effect, take over another room. Things were looking better all the time.

Jason felt as if he were hiding away, getting all his possessions together, awaiting the conflict that was about to come, digging himself in, sheltering in his bunker.

When he had all his CDs and stereo in the bedroom, he sat on his bed and sank into misery. He felt like ringing Heather and telling her what was going on, but the phone was down in the hall and he wouldn't want Karl to hear. Maybe he could go out to a phone box and call her. Yes, that sounded like a good idea. Get him away from Karl as well.

Jason picked up his wallet and doorkeys and walked downstairs. He checked that the basement door was locked and then stepped outside. It was a bright sunny day, and it cheered him up straight away. He turned left and walked past his neighbours' quiet houses, then through an estate of comfortable semi-detached houses, and on to the road that led into Woodvale town centre. He found a call box next to a garage, and dialled Heather's number. He usually spoke to her about once a week on the phone, so it wasn't anything unusual to ring her. She wasn't in, though. He let the phone ring about fifteen times and then gave up.

Not wanting to go back to the house, he carried on towards the shops. He could visit the small record store, see if they had anything reduced, and then go to the Ancient House bookshop, a small old building with beams on the ceiling, to see if they had anything of interest. Record shops and bookshops. It felt like he'd spent his whole life going into them.

After setting up his stereo in the living room, Karl drove the Fiesta Azura a hundred yards up the road and parked outside an off-licence. He marched inside and bought four crates of beer, six one-and-a-half litre bottles of wine, two bottles of vodka, some soft drinks, and various packets of crisps and nuts. He managed to negotiate a 10 per cent discount on the wine – no luck with the beer and vodka – paid in cash, and then got one of the staff to help him load up. He drove the Azura home and started unloading.

He carried the drink into the kitchen and opened the fridge. All the shelves inside were packed with Jason's food. There were yogurts, cheeses, vegetables, half a bottle of wine, and lots of other things in paper bags and tin-foil wrappings. Karl swore. How the fuck was he going to get all the booze in?

He walked down the hall and shouted up the stairs for Jason. No answer. He walked to the basement stairs and shouted down. Nothing.

Back in the kitchen, he found a black bin liner, and started taking all of Jason's food out of the fridge and dropping it in. He put the bin bag on top of the kitchen counter, and now surveyed an empty fridge.

He ripped open the shrink-wraps of beer and started piling the cans inside. He thought he'd better put some wine in there, too, but couldn't remember if it was white or red that you were meant to chill. He stuck in one of each.

He closed the fridge door and put the remaining drink on the counter next to the bin liner. He would just have to replenish the fridge as it emptied.

Feeling satisfied with his morning's work, he went upstairs to the bathroom and started running a bath. There was a shower in there, too, he was pleased to see, but a nice long soak was what he needed, get his body smelling pretty in case he got lucky tonight. As he got undressed he wondered who would turn up. He had made a few phone calls yesterday and expected a good turn-out. Slightly more than the four or five he had told Jason about.

After spending a couple of hours in Woodvale, Jason started wandering back home. He was clutching a second-hand copy of *No One Here Gets Out Alive*, a biography of Jim Morrison he had always wanted to read. He had found it in one of the second-hand bookshops next to the Ancient House. He stopped by another call box and tried Heather's number again, but still no luck.

When he got home it was after two o'clock and time for lunch. He walked into the kitchen and opened the fridge.

Karl was soaking in the bath when he heard the banging on the door.

'Karl, are you in there?'

It was Jason and he sounded angry.

'Having a bath, my man. What's up?' Karl said through the steam.

'Where's all the food from the fridge? You haven't thrown it out have you?'

'Of course not. Have a look in the bin bag. It's all in there.'

'How the hell do you expect it to stay fresh in a bin bag?'

'It'll only be there a few hours,' Karl said. 'You can put it back after the party. In fact, I'll put it back for you myself.'

'It's about eighty degrees outside. I don't think it's going to stay fresh that long.'

Karl was starting to get annoyed. Who was this wimp? Why all this fuss over a bit of food? He climbed out of the bath and unlocked the door. Standing wet and naked in front of Jason he said, 'What is your problem, Jason?'

Jason felt uneasy staring at a naked Karl. He knew Karl was doing it to throw him off guard. He could sense a large penis hanging there, but he was determined not to look at it.

'You can't just empty my fridge of food. I'm not rolling in money you know.'

'So money's the problem, is it?'

Jason shook his head. 'The principle's the problem. It's courteous to ask someone before you touch their belongings.'

'I came to ask you,' Karl said, 'but you were out.'

'You could've waited until I got back.'

'I didn't know if you were coming back.'

'My car's still outside. I couldn't have got far.'

'Jesus fucking Christ!'

Then Karl pushed his way past him and into his bedroom. Jason stood on the landing wondering what he'd gone to get. A knife? A gun?

But Karl came back with a ten-pound note in his hand.

'Here,' he said. 'Take this. That should cover anything that goes off.'

Jason took the money and stood to one side so Karl could go back to the bathroom. The door slammed shut behind him. Jason felt pleased with himself as he went downstairs, happy that he'd stood up to Karl and got a tenner out of it as well. That would easily cover whatever food rotted.

By eight o'clock Karl was ready to party. He was dressed in a white collarless shirt, black leather jeans and black boots. He studied himself in the full-length mirror on his wardrobe door and thought, This is as cool as a man can get.

He left his bedroom and saw that the door to Jason's room was shut. He knocked softly on the door.

'Jason, are you in there?'

The door opened to reveal Jason, still in his shorts. The door to his balcony was open and Karl could see a bottle of red wine and a glass on the floor, next to a chair. Some sort of wimpy music flowed softly out of the room.

'Having a good time?' Karl asked.

'A fine time,' Jason said. 'Another bottle of wine and I'll be feeling even finer.'

'You ought to slow down a bit. The party hasn't started yet.'

'I'm not much of a party-goer. I'll just stay in my room.'

Karl nodded. He thought as much. 'Well, if you change your mind, just come down. There should be some spare women.'

'I'll see how I feel.'

'OK. See you later.'

Karl went downstairs and got a cool beer from the fridge. He noticed that the bin liner of food was gone. Jason probably had it in his room so no one else would touch it. Maybe he was going to eat all of it tonight before it went off.

Karl opened one of the cupboards and took out various dishes and plates. He opened packets of crisps and nuts and tipped them out. Then he carried them into the living room.

The living room had pink wall-to-wall carpet with several rugs on top. Karl rolled up the rugs and dropped them behind the settee that he'd already moved against the front window. He pushed the two armchairs up to the wall in case anyone wanted to dance, and noticed that Jason had also taken his TV and video away. After putting some soul music on the CD player he sat in an armchair nibbling crisps. He wondered who would be the first to arrive. Most people would wait until the pubs shut but he didn't care too much. He had a whole fridge full of booze to keep him company.

After one bottle of red wine things didn't seem so bleak to Jason. Sitting on the balcony, looking out over his garden and the back gardens of the houses opposite, eating food from the black bin liner, Jackson Browne on the stereo behind him in the bedroom. When he was halfway through the second bottle things seemed fairly rosy. It was still quiet downstairs and he was thinking maybe Karl's friends weren't going to turn up and the whole evening would be wasted. He was hoping that's what would happen, take Karl down a peg or two.

He watched the sun sink below the horizon, and by around nine o'clock it had started getting dark. He could hear music from downstairs, but not too loud, a few voices, but no one shouting or being silly. He brought his things in from the balcony and closed the glass doors. He lay down on his bed and carried on reading *No One Here Gets Out Alive*.

71

Then he closed his eyes.

His eyes felt heavy.

Then he fell asleep.

A deep red-wine sleep.

He dreamed of Heather: he was kissing her down in the basement. Jason had his trousers undone but not much else was happening. Then Heather shaved all her hair off. She suddenly looked like Sinead O'Connor. Jason woke up.

He looked over at the bedside clock. It was two in the morning. There was a thumping going on in his head. There was a thumping coming from downstairs as well. The house had come alive.

Jason took his aching bladder to the toilet at the end of the landing. He was glad there was another one downstairs so he wouldn't get people trooping up here all night. But the toilet was locked.

He walked back down the hall to the bathroom and turned on the light. There was a short blond guy in there pissing in the sink.

'Jesus Christ!' Jason said. 'What the hell are you doing?'

The bloke looked back over his shoulder. 'Pissing in the sink,' he said and laughed.

Jason shook his head. He didn't have the energy to argue. And wasn't that what he'd come in to do? 'Well, make sure you wash it away,' he said, then walked back to wait outside the toilet.

The toilet flushed a minute later and a girl in her early twenties came out. He said hello to her and introduced himself. She seemed a little drunk to him, but was quite pretty.

'I haven't see you before,' she said. 'Are you coming down to the party?'

'I don't think so,' Jason said. 'I'm feeling a little tired.'

'Come on, it'll do you good,' the girl said. Then she started walking away. 'I'll be waiting for you,' she said over her shoulder, and then giggled.

Jason went into the toilet and felt a little lighter when he walked out. He decided to go downstairs to see if he could find the girl. But first he went back to his room and changed out of his shorts.

Karl saw Jason standing in the doorway to the living room, and thought, Wonders will never cease. He took his hand out of the blouse of the girl next to him on the sofa and staggered over to greet him.

'Jason, my man!' he shouted over the music. 'You're a bit late, but I'm glad you made it.'

Jason was smiling at him, and looked a little pissed to Karl. He was holding a can of lager.

'I went to the fridge,' Jason shouted, 'but all I could find in there was booze!' He started laughing and Karl clapped him on the back.

'Let me introduce you to some people,' he said.

Jason let himself be introduced. The loud disco music was nearly bursting his brain, and there were several couples dancing in there, while ten or twelve people stood around talking. They were all younger than Jason, but didn't look a bad crowd. He didn't know why he'd been so uptight about the situation. He half regretted he hadn't come down earlier, although he hadn't been lying when he'd said parties weren't his scene. He looked for the pretty girl from upstairs but couldn't see her anywhere.

Karl was walking him round the room, and Jason was shaking hands and smiling and not remembering a single name. When they'd toured the whole room they finally came to a couple who had just walked in the door. The girl had long dark hair, and the bloke had short hair and a goatee like half the blokes Jason had just been introduced to. There were so many men with goatees these days, and they all looked the same. Jason wondered who or what had started this craze. He was damned if he knew.

He found himself reaching out and shaking two more hands. The guy with the goatee reached out a massive paw and crushed him with a vice-like grip. Jason said, 'Ouch!' and backed off.

'My name's Phil,' the guy said. 'My friends just call me Goatee, though.'

Jason started laughing.

'What's so funny?' Phil said.

'Your friends call you Goatee,' Jason said. 'That's pretty funny.'

Now the guy was looking at him seriously. 'They don't call me Goatee,' he said. 'They call me Gator.'

Jason noticed the look and apologized. 'It's the music,' he said. 'I can't hear a damn thing in here.'

But the guy called Gator wasn't really listening. He was already walking past Jason into the living room.

9

On Sunday morning Jesse Morgan was out jogging in Woodvale Priory. He was dressed in shorts, a running vest and Asics trainers, and had a hangover. He had spent the best part of the previous evening watching TV, downing half a bottle of whisky while sitting through a made-for-TV crime film starring Brian Dennehy, and then a so-called comedy show. He had enjoyed neither, his mind wandering to Nicola, replaying parts of their conversation from the Friday night. He knew she could be the best thing to happen to him in years.

He was running his usual circuit of the priory – about a three-mile run. He did this at least three times a week, not because he was any kind of physical-fitness freak, but mostly to counter his drinking habit. He drank regularly every evening after work – wine with his meal and then whisky afterwards – and though he was no alcoholic, he drank more than was healthy for a man his age. He felt that sweating it off three times a week was a good way of countering the alcohol's ill-effects, or at least of keeping trim. It was also a tonic for the mind.

As he ran he was thinking of Frankie Bosser, and hoping maybe something exciting would finally happen in Woodvale. The crime rate in the area was so low his job was more like that of a social worker these days. He would stick it out until the end of the year and then ask for a transfer back to London. But, then again, if things started happening with Nicola, would he want to move back? He would have to wait and see.

Detective Sergeant Ian Kiddie and a couple of others had been keeping watch at the Bosser house for the past few days, but so far all was quiet. Daniela Bosser had been coming and going as normal, and there had been no sign as yet of her stepson. The main airports had been alerted as well, in case he decided not to hang around for the funeral after all. But there were so many small airports in England, Bosser could sneak out more or less when he wanted. All he needed to do was turn up with a wad of cash and hand it over to some unscrupulous pilot. It was easily done. It had happened before. And from what Morgan knew, he was sure Bosser had more than a small wad of cash available.

Morgan started up a steep incline, two hundred yards of sheer torture. He struggled past young couples with prams and old people out with their dogs. They looked at him as if he were mad; maybe he was. When he reached the top he had to stop for a few minutes to catch his breath. It was a good view from here: distant woods and fields, not many houses in sight – England's green and pleasant land. When he felt slightly better he jogged slowly along a dirt footpath, still getting his breath back, and then turned left down the slope. This part was total pleasure, the nearest thing to flying a human could get – without a hang-glider. Morgan was down the hill in seconds, a mere blur to the morning walkers. Then he was on the flat of the playing fields, slowing down now, jogging past goalposts without their nets, redundant until the football season started once again. And then he saw Nicola jogging slowly towards him.

Nicola was dressed in skimpy running shorts, a Bart Simpson T-shirt and cheap trainers without any socks. She hardly ever went jogging but had seen Jesse from her living-room window and had decided to go looking for him. By the time she had changed and run out to the priory, though, he had disappeared. She decided to do some stretches and wait, in the hope that he would run back her way.

Ten minutes later she saw him charging down a slope in the distance, and then he was running in her direction. He looked impressive to her with an athletic, smooth running action. He slowed down as he reached her and she saw he had a wide grin on his face.

'You're not a jogger as well, are you?' he asked when he'd stopped. He bent over double, trying to get his breath back.

'I saw you from my flat,' Nicola said. 'I thought you might need some help recovering.'

'I may need the kiss of life in a minute.'

'That could be fun,' Nicola said.

Then he stood upright, streams of sweat running off his face, still breathing heavily. Nicola looked at his shoulders and arms. Good muscles: hard and sinewy. She felt like squeezing them.

'You look in great shape,' she said, 'but you don't sound it.'

'I'm all right until I stop,' he said. 'Then I sound like a heavy smoker. Let's walk the rest of the way.'

He took her by the arm and they headed back towards the car park.

'I thought I might see you in the pub last night,' Nicola said.

'I wanted to come, but I don't like hanging around bars on my own.'

'You could have chatted to me.'

'You would've been working. I might have distracted you.'

'You would have.' She gave him a playful nudge.

'So you're not a jogger?' he asked her.

'Is it that obvious?'

Jesse laughed. 'You've got the physique, but not the technique.'

'Are you a poet as well?'

'Only on Sundays.'

'Actually, I don't think it's good for you. All that pounding of the body. It can cause you harm in the long term, you know.'

'How?'

'Think how many times your feet hit the ground. All that impact. All that weight. It jars the bones. It may lead to arthritis in later years. Or hip problems.'

'You're sure about this, are you?'

'I read health magazines. I do what I can to stay fit.'

'And what do you do?'

'A bit of stretching. A bit of yoga. And a bit of tennis.'

'Well, I could play you at tennis some time. I used to play a bit in school, but not that much since.'

'You're on. They have courts just over there.' Nicola pointed to a row of six tarmac courts. Then she felt silly because Jesse would know they were over there.

'We'll book a game some time,' he said, his breath now sounding normal.

Then he was inspecting the front of her T-shirt. Nicola felt embarrassed. She thought he was looking at her breasts. That was another reason she didn't jog. She didn't like her boobs swinging every which way. She was glad she'd put on a bra before coming out.

'Who's that on your shirt?' asked Jesse.

Nicola laughed with relief. 'Bart Simpson. A cartoon character.'

'You're into cartoons?'

'Not really. It's on TV. It's the only cartoon I watch. A show called *The Simpsons*. It's very funny.'

'I don't watch kids' shows.'

'It's not a kids' show!'

'He looks demented. He looks like a few people I've arrested in my time.'

Nicola laughed. 'He's not demented, he's cute.'

'I'll take your word for it.'

They were at the car park now and Jesse was walking towards his car.

'Are you going home now?' Nicola asked.

Jesse nodded. 'I usually just drive home like this and then jump in the shower.'

'Would you like to shower at my place and then have some breakfast?'

'I don't have any clothes with me, just a tracksuit.'

'So change into your tracksuit. No one's going to see.'

'OK. Wait a second.'

Nicola watched Jesse walk to his car, unlock it, and bring out a sportsbag. He slung it on his shoulder and they walked off towards her flat.

'Shall we get some Sunday papers?' she asked.

'Only if you've got a week to spare.'

'I'll buy the *Mail on Sunday*. That's the only one I can handle. It doesn't have too many sections.'

'Lead the way.'

Morgan couldn't believe all this was happening so quickly, perhaps too quickly for him. He hadn't had a serious relationship for four years, and now in the space of a few days it looked like he was embarking on one. As he waited outside the newsagent's the first verse of a country song came into his head. It went:

> *I haven't loved a woman for four years,*
> *Haven't even kissed one goodnight,*
> *And all my thoughts of failure*
> *Recur as I turn out the light.*
> *My bed's a straitjacket of freedom*
> *Measuring three feet wide,*
> *And the lonely nights just get longer*
> *When you've got no one at your side.*

'What's that you're singing?' Nicola had come up behind without him noticing.

'Was I singing?' Morgan said uncomfortably.

'Well, humming might be more accurate.'

They started walking towards her flat.

'It's a country song called "Make Mine A Double". I can't remember who sang it.'

Nicola shook her head. 'I've never heard of it.'

'The chorus goes: "This time make mine a double, give me all the drink that I need, I promise not to cause any trouble, it's the only way I'll be freed."'

'I still don't know it. Is that something you relate to?' Nicola asked.

'Too much recently, I'm afraid,' he said.

They reached the entrance to Nicola's flat and Morgan followed her up the stairs. He studied her legs for the first time. Slim and well shaped, no excess fat. Her shorts were so tiny he caught a glimpse of her knickers. Pale blue.

'Getting a good view?' she asked over her shoulder.

'Terrific,' he said.

When they were in her flat she led him into the bathroom and gave him a clean towel. The shower was in a cubicle next to the sink. She showed him how to work the controls and he needed a lot of willpower not to take her in his arms and undress her right there. His head was spinning with emotion. Then she left him alone and he started to strip off his sweaty running clothes.

In the shower, as he soaped, he could feel himself getting hard. He turned his back to the glass door and thought he'd better relieve himself or he'd be on edge all the way through breakfast. He leaned against the wall and started rubbing himself, thinking of Nicola's legs as he'd followed her up the stairs.

Karl was gradually coming awake on Sunday morning in his double bed. His head was throbbing and he dared not open his eyes, but he could feel a weight on the bed next to him. He couldn't remember who'd got into bed with him. He would have to open his eyes some time, just to check out who the mystery person was. He had screwed a girl called Bobbie at about three o'clock in this very bed, but he was sure he hadn't invited her up to sleep with him. In fact, hadn't he told her to get lost when he'd finished with her? Maybe it was another girl and he could get an early morning screw when she woke up. He turned over, forcing his eyes open. The body next to him was Gator, lying there naked!

Karl jumped out of bed and Gator sleepily opened his eyes at the commotion.

'What the fuck're you doing in my bed?' Karl asked, standing in his boxer shorts.

'This your bed?' Gator said, not in the real world yet.

'You know fucking well it is! I know you've been away a long time, but you aren't getting my arse.'

Now Gator was awake. 'Fuck off, Karl. I got my end away last night, if you really want to know. This was the only sleeping area that wasn't taken. Go downstairs and have a look. There are bodies everywhere.'

'Jesus!' said Karl. 'You'd better tell people you slept on the floor, not in my bed.'

'If you like, you uptight shithead.'

Karl went to the window and drew back the curtains with a violent sweep. He and Gator both moaned as the light hit them, and Gator pulled the duvet over his head.

Karl scampered downstairs and had a look in the living room. Sure enough, there were bodies everywhere, some of them entangled, some on their own. The room looked like a grenade had hit it, cans and ashtrays on the floor, sleeping-bags like body-bags, and pieces of clothing. Karl went to the kitchen and put on the kettle.

When he'd made two cups of tea he carried them gingerly back upstairs. The door to Jason's room was slightly open and Karl nudged it further with his foot. There was a girl lying naked in bed, a nice pair of tits showing above the sheets. Karl felt like jumping in with her, but then he noticed another body with her: Jason. He chuckled and went back to his room.

'Well, Jason got some, too,' he said to Gator. 'I didn't think he had it in him.'

'Who the fuck's Jason?' asked Gator, his voice muffled under the duvet.

'The owner of this house, dickhead. The owner of the very bed you're lying in.'

'The square oik with the glasses?'

'That's him. Here's a cup of tea.'

Karl placed the tea on the bedside table, then rummaged through an unpacked box for some aspirin. He ripped open the silver foil and dropped two into his mouth. He gave two to Gator who was now sitting up in bed sipping his tea.

'So who did you screw?' asked Karl. 'Wendy?'

'Yeah.'

'Where did you do it? Not here in the bed while I was sleeping, I hope.'

Gator shook his head. 'On the back lawn. Behind some bushes.'

'You always had style.'

'It's amazing what you can get away with in this world.'

They drank their tea in silence for a while. Karl looked out at the quiet street below, lots of cars and a few motorbikes belonging to the people who'd stayed overnight. No doubt Jason would be getting some complaints from neighbours later.

'On the subject of getting away with things,' Karl said. 'Are we going to do another job together?' It was Karl who had driven the getaway car for Gator when he'd pulled the petrol-station robbery three months ago, the job that had forced Gator to flee to Europe. Karl had stayed behind because he didn't have a police record so there was no way they'd come looking for him. He had found the whole thing very exciting and now had a desire for more. As long as he didn't get caught, of course. That would be a complete disaster.

Now he had Gator's complete attention. 'Got the taste for it now, have you?'

'It's a nice way to supplement my income.'

'What did you have in mind?'

Karl sipped his tea. 'I've been casing out a post office in Orton. It's so behind the times it looks like an easy one to me. Want to go and have a look at it?'

Gator stroked his goatee and then ran his fingers through the hair on his chest. 'What else is there to do on a Sunday?' he said.

10

By the time Monday rolled around, Frankie Bosser was getting restless and felt like flying home to Italy. His search for the killer of his father had led nowhere and didn't look like progressing any further. After all, he was no private detective, and after his chat to Joe in the Railway he didn't have a clue where else to look. He could hardly wander the streets of Woodvale looking for a long-haired traveller carrying a rucksack. So he had spent long periods of the weekend sitting in his hotel room, watching TV and reading, and doing sit-ups and press-ups. He wished he had brought some running gear with him so he could burn off some energy. The only time he had left his room was to take a couple of drives in the Sierra, one on each day of the weekend.

On the Saturday he had driven to Nutfield, the village of his childhood, which was about three miles away from Redgate. He'd parked outside the house he'd been brought up in, and walked up the drive for a look. The house had been named Sentinels when he was a child, but now it was called the Abode. Frankie hated the name. When he knocked on the door there was no answer. He walked round the garden looking at the two-storey house which now had light pink walls. Lots of childhood memories flooded through his head. On the lawn he used to play football on his own, and he'd even made his own putting green, nine holes that he'd dug out around the edges of the front and back gardens. He had been a solitary boy, wasting many hours on his own, living out sporting fantasies, waiting for his father to come back from work so they could have a kickaround together. But walking around the garden on Saturday, thinking about his father, Frankie started feeling despondent, so he left after about five minutes and returned to his car.

He drove around Nutfield, looking at other haunts. First the local church where he'd gone every Sunday with his parents. He chuckled to himself at the thought of going in there now; would they even let him through the door? Then he stopped outside the Vine pub, where he'd often sat in his father's Rover with a soft drink and a packet of crisps, while his parents were drinking inside. Next he drove down Proctor Street and took a look at an old friend's house. Two brothers had lived there, the Ashbys, and Frankie had learned at the age of eighteen about the death of Stephen, the elder, killed in a motorcycle accident. Stephen was the first person Frankie had known who had died. It had shocked him at the time and still made him sad to think of it. Here he was at the age of forty-one, the same age Stephen would be now, and he'd had twenty-three years' more living than him, with more to come. Where was the justice in that? It was all down to luck.

All the reminiscing had been enough for one day, so Frankie had driven back to the hotel, ordered a late lunch from room service, and sat in his room watching black and white films on TV. In the late afternoon he had walked to a nearby newsagent and bought a reduced-price paperback by someone called Elmore Leonard. The novel was called *Glitz* and it was about a middle-aged cop tracking down the psycho who had killed his girlfriend. Frankie could find parallels to the situation he was in, but the guy in the book was having a lot more success than he was and knew the right way to go about tracking down someone. Frankie didn't think he'd find the killer of his father, but the book gave him some kind of hope. He finished it at eleven o'clock, then tumbled into bed.

On Sunday he drove down to his old cottage in Burmarsh, where he had shot the policeman on that terrible night. He stood on the street and looked over the hedge. The house seemed the same, but now there were a couple of kids playing in the half-acre of garden. There were two cars in the drive, slightly less than when Frankie had been there; he'd always had at least five vehicles parked around the place. His business had been wound down by Malcolm, his accountant, the vehicles sold, the left-over booze divided up among his four employees. The police had questioned Malcolm about Frankie's whereabouts, but Malcolm didn't know himself, so couldn't tell them a thing. The money from the car and van sales had then been passed on to Frankie's father, who had sent it out to Italy by various means, usually through friends of Daniela when they visited Courmayeur.

Frankie then drove further into Burmarsh and had a cup of tea in one of the cafés. The village looked exactly the same, no development. He read a Sunday newspaper and looked out of the window at passing families.

For the rest of the day he just drove around, stopping at a pub for supper, then heading back to the hotel for the evening. He liked touring the English countryside, but wished someone like Veronica were there with him. He realized he did miss England, but felt on edge all the time now, as though someone might recognize him and turn him in. He didn't know if he was just being paranoid or overcautious. After all, how much of a wanted man was he? Maybe he was wanted in Burmarsh and Woodvale but he was hardly Ronnie Biggs or Lord Lucan. He wasn't wanted by the whole of Britain. As long as he kept a low profile he was sure he'd be all right.

On the way back to Redgate Frankie passed through Godstone, the village where his stepfather now lived. His mother had died of cancer before Frankie had left England and he hadn't spoken to his stepfather since. He wasn't about to start now.

Back in the hotel room by Sunday evening, Frankie started another Elmore Leonard novel, *La Brava*, a second-hand copy he'd found in the hotel lounge. It was just as good as *Glitz* and made the hours fly by. He wasn't usually much of a reader – he hardly had the time for it – but he was enjoying this new pastime. Maybe he could keep it up when he got back to Italy.

On Monday he was still feeling restless, so he left the Sierra at the hotel and went for a walk around Redgate, the first time he'd dared to since his arrival, nearly a week ago. He walked under the bridge by the railway station, and wandered round the Belfry shopping centre looking for faces he recognized. In the old days he couldn't walk through Redgate or Woodvale without bumping into someone he knew. Would that still be the case?

After the excesses of Saturday night Jason had spent most of Sunday recovering. He hadn't felt well enough to leave his bed until just after three in the afternoon. Sally, the girl he'd slept with, had already disappeared. She'd kissed him goodbye and left her phone number on a piece of paper. By the time Jason felt well enough to rise, the house was empty. Karl had cleared up all the mess from the living room, and the booze had vanished from the fridge. Jason took the bin liner from his bedroom and put all his food back.

By Monday he was back to his normal self. He was feeling uplifted by his night of drunken sex, and felt in the mood to give Sally a ring later in the evening. First, though, he had to drive into Redgate to buy some guitar strings. He jumped into his Mini, and drove away from 8 Naughton Road.

Parking in Redgate for free was always something of a challenge, and one that Jason looked forward to. Redgate was predominantly a commuter town, a thirty-minute train ride into central London, and all the streets surrounding the station were packed with commuters' cars. This annoyed all the local residents, but Jason reasoned that if you wanted to live near a station then that was the price you paid. In his Mini, though, he could squeeze into spaces that bigger cars couldn't even contemplate. He would drive round the side streets until he found such a space, back in with consummate ease and wander away smugly.

Now he was heading for the Redgate Guitar Centre. It was down a small side street, slightly off the main shopping area and was run by two guys called Julian and Dave. Julian was the person Jason dealt with most of the time, a talkative chap in his mid-thirties with wavy hair and glasses. He also made guitars, and filled most of his days repairing and tinkering. Dave was a guitar teacher, taking lessons in the back of the shop. Jason reckoned that between himself and Dave they had most of the guitar tutoring in the Redgate/Woodvale area sewn up.

Jason bought a new set of D'Addario strings for his black Takamine guitar, and left after a fifteen-minute chat with Julian. He wondered where to go next. Then, walking towards him past the row of shops on the right, he saw a man who looked slightly familiar. Jason stood where he was and waited for the man to come nearer. As he approached, he looked towards Jason and there was recognition on his face too. They were staring at each other now, the man crossing the side street and then walking right up to Jason. He stopped a yard away and smiled.

'I know your face,' the man said. 'Fuller's Earth factory, about twenty years ago. Do you remember me?'

Jason searched his memory for a name. He knew he recognized the man, but twenty years was a long time. 'You look familiar,' he said warily. 'You worked at Fuller's Earth?'

'Yeah. Frankie Bosser. You used to sing in the Station Hotel.' Now the man was pointing at Jason's chest, looking genuinely pleased to see him. 'You used to play guitar and sing folk songs. I was thinking about you only the other day. You used to get on the stage and blow everyone away. An excellent singer. I always thought you'd make it. Did you?'

Jason had to laugh. 'Not exactly. I make money from playing, but I've never become a star. It's all a bit of a struggle at the minute, actually.'

Now the man called Frankie was shaking his head. 'You know, I thought I'd take a walk around Redgate this morning. I'm just here for a few days. I said to myself, I wonder if I can walk round and recognize someone so many years after living here, and bingo! Nothing ever changes, does it?'

Jason looked at the streets and shops. 'Not really, no. Except for the car parks. They're always building more of those.'

Frankie was still shaking his head in disbelief. 'You know you've made my day. I've been getting really bored sitting in my hotel room. How about a drink to fill in the missing years?'

Jason looked at his watch and noticed he still had an hour or so before his first lesson. He nodded at Frankie. 'OK,' he said. 'I've got an hour to spare. This pub next door's all right.'

'Great!' Frankie said, and Jason felt pleased that someone was so glad to see him.

He followed Frankie into the pub, walking behind the six-footer with the broad shoulders. At the bar Frankie reached in his trouser pocket and pulled out a thick roll of twenty-pound notes. Jason's eyes nearly popped out. First Karl and his roll of money, and now Frankie. He must be doing something wrong with his life. Frankie turned and smiled at Jason. 'What can I get you?'

'I'll have a glass of dry white wine,' Jason said. He was surprised to see Frankie order a mineral water for himself. He had only ordered the wine to be sociable and would've preferred a soft drink himself after the weekend's excesses. But it was too late now. They went to sit at a table.

The pub was fairly full with office workers and residents from the nearby flats. Jason took a sip of his wine and asked Frankie what he'd been doing with his life.

'After leaving Fuller's Earth,' Frankie said, 'I became a card salesman, if you remember. Driving up and down the country all week, staying in bed and breakfasts. I loved the travelling for a while but after six years I got a little sick of it.'

'What did you do after that?'

'I became self-employed. I became an importer of booze from France.'

'You mean loading up a car and coming back to sell it in England? Isn't that illegal?'

Frankie shrugged. 'Well, it's not strictly legal. It's a bit of an opportunity, is what it is. Unfortunately, nowadays everyone is doing it. They'll have to put a stop to it somehow. Change some laws.'

'So you still do that? All these years later?'

Frankie shook his head. 'I made a bunch of money and got out. I bought a stake in a bar in Italy, and that's where I live now.'

'Sounds nice.'

'It is. It's a ski resort, so it's very lively in the winter. Summers are a bit quieter. Just a load of walkers.'

'So you're back here on holiday?'

'A funeral. My father died last week so I've flown over for that.'

'I'm sorry,' Jason said.

'These things happen.'

Jason nodded. He envied the man sitting opposite him. Obviously making a lot of money, living in a pretty village in Europe. He could do with some of that himself. Would he be a struggling guitar teacher all his life, always scratching to make a living?

'How about you?' Frankie asked. 'What happened when you left the Earth?'

'Well,' Jason said, 'I basically went straight into teaching. I saved quite a bit while I was at the factory, and I took a year off and got my lessons going. Then I played in a band as well and that brought in some extra money. We played a lot of weddings and functions. I've been to so many weddings but never my own.' Jason laughed to cover his sadness.

'That's no big deal,' Frankie said. 'I've never been married either. I think it's overrated myself. Talk to most married men and they're as miserable as sin.'

'You could be right.'

'I know I'm right.'

Jason watched Frankie drinking his water.

'So that's what you've been doing ever since?' asked Frankie.

'Yeah. It's been one long picnic,' Jason said sarcastically.

'I always thought you'd become famous,' Frankie said. 'Haven't you ever tried to make a record?'

'I've made demos, sent them to record companies. Never had any interest. I think I've found my proper level.'

'So you're not making much money, I take it?'

'Never a fortune. Just enough to get by, a carrot to keep me interested. The trouble is I don't know how to do anything else. Then, to cap it all, my girlfriend left a few months ago. And now I've had to take a lodger into my house to help pay the mortgage.'

'And the lodger's an arsehole?'

'He's a bit weird,' said Jason. 'I haven't passed final judgement on him yet. We're definitely not made for each other, though.' He chuckled and got a sympathetic look from Frankie. It was good to be able to talk about his problems with someone. This was the first decent conversation he'd had with anyone since Heather left.

'Well, we all have to adapt to our situation,' Frankie said. 'Another drink?'

Thirty minutes later Frankie was sitting hunched up in Jason's Mini, trying to get comfortable. Minis were never designed for six-footers.

They were driving back to Jason's place so he could take his first lesson of the day. Frankie would walk round Woodvale for an hour and then go back and see him afterwards. Hear him play some music.

When Jason parked outside his house there was already someone waiting by the front door: a young girl sitting with a guitar case.

'Your lesson?' asked Frankie.

'Yeah. She's a sweetie. Always on time. Always practises hard. She's a rarity.'

'I'll leave you to it, then,' said Frankie, climbing awkwardly out of the car. 'I'll see you in an hour or so.' He wandered off towards the town centre.

In the old days Frankie had been as likely to bump into someone he knew in Woodvale as in Redgate. He was feeling pleased that he'd met Jason. They seemed to get on well, and another pleasing fact was that Jason didn't seem to know about

Frankie's shady past and the dead policeman. Maybe Frankie was being paranoid and nobody knew or cared who he was. All of a sudden he felt that his trip home was brightening up. Maybe he could kill some time with Jason until some progress was made about his father's funeral. If, that is, anything did ever start to happen about the funeral. Frankie could only give it another week and then would have to consider going back to Italy. In fact, now would be a good time to give Daniela a ring and see if there was any news. He found a phone box and dialled the number.

'No, nothing new is happening,' Daniela said, when she'd picked up the phone. 'I pester the police every day. Soon they will give in, I hope. And how are you, Frankie?'

Frankie told her about bumping into Jason, and said he might try to socialize a bit, maybe get out more because he was getting restless at the hotel.

'Well don't socialize too much, Frankie,' said Daniela. 'We don't want people recognizing you.'

Frankie told her he would be careful.

For the next hour Frankie looked in shop windows in the town centre. He was amazed to see some of the shops still there after so long, but there were lots of new buildings as well, the biggest being the new cinema, which was now a triple-screen instead of the single one Frankie could remember taking girls to. He didn't know any of the films playing there.

When his hour was up Frankie walked slowly back towards Jason's house. As he approached the front gate he saw a big guy standing next to one of the three cars in the drive. He seemed to be talking to someone but Frankie couldn't see anyone else. Jason had told him a bit about Karl in the pub, and Frankie took this to be him. He walked over to the man and said, 'Are you Karl?'

Karl turned with suspicion in his eyes, gave Frankie the once over, and said, 'Who wants to know?'

Frankie held out his hand and said, 'I'm a friend of Jason. Frankie's the name.'

Karl reluctantly turned towards Frankie and shook his hand.

Frankie was ready to give him the Bosser grip, show him who was in charge, but Karl's handshake was weak, like a woman's.

'Are these all your cars?' Frankie asked.

'They might be,' Karl said cagily.

Frankie had to smile. Karl looked tough but he'd met a hundred like him before. Maybe he could intimidate Jason with his antics, but he didn't fool Frankie for a minute.

'I might be in the market for a car,' Frankie lied. 'What are the prices of these three?'

Karl told him and Frankie feigned interest. They walked around the three cars until Frankie saw some legs poking out from underneath the Fiat.

'You've got a corpse underneath that one,' he said. 'I hope you're not charging extra for it.'

Karl didn't seem to find that funny. 'That's my mechanic,' he said. 'I'd introduce you but he's probably got a face full of oil.'

'What's his name?' Frankie asked.

'His friends call him Gator,' Karl said. 'Best mechanic I've ever had.'

Frankie nodded. 'I'll take your word for it. Is Jason in?'

'Go to the basement door at the back. Down the stairs,' Karl said. 'Jason spends all his time down there.'

'And you spend all yours out here, right?' Frankie said, but Karl didn't have an answer to that. Frankie walked past him and then had to step over Gator's legs to get to the basement door. Well, he thought to himself. This is more entertaining than sitting in the hotel.

11

On Tuesday, his second day as a fork-lift driver for Ellis Pipes, Phil Gator knew he'd landed on his feet, even though at the moment he was lying on his back. His new job was ridiculously easy, he'd got laid at the weekend by Wendy and he and Karl were looking into the possibility of robbing the post office over in the small village of Orton. Things were moving along nicely since he'd returned home.

Today the sun was beating down out of a clear blue sky, and Gator was sunbathing on a stack of pallets in the yard, waiting for someone to come out of the office and give him something to do. Yesterday, he had spent most of the time on the fork-lift, rearranging the yard while Brian the foreman gave directions from the rubbled ground. Mr Carroll had surfaced from the office a few times to give his point of view, but Gator had ignored him. He didn't have any time for upper-class twits like that.

After about an hour of browning his skin, Gator heard the door to the Portakabin opening to his right. He turned his head and saw Brian walking over. He sat up and said, 'Are we on the move?'

Brian nodded. 'There's a lorry on its way. A big order, apparently.'

Gator stood up and stretched. Brian was looking at his bare top. Gator was already bronzed from his months in Europe and he had to admit to himself he was a fine-looking specimen.

'You've got a good tan,' Brian said. 'I wish I could lie out here all day.'

'What do you do in the office, then?' Gator asked, just to make conversation.

'A bit of paperwork. Filling in charts and graphs. Anything to look busy, really.'

'Is it always this quiet?'

'At the moment. It should get busier, though. The last driver left because it was too quiet.'

'Now you tell me.'

'Some people like quiet jobs. You don't mind lying in the sun, do you?'

'I might after a few weeks.'

'You can top up that tan of yours.' Brian was looking at Gator's body again.

Gator felt uneasy. 'You're not a queer are you?' he asked.

Brian laughed nervously. 'I'm a married man,' he said.

'That doesn't make much difference these days.'

Gator reached for his T-shirt and put it on. 'Let's get one thing straight,' he said. 'I'm no butt fucker, and if you are, I'd appreciate it if you kept your eyes and your hands to yourself. Otherwise you'll be looking pretty quickly for another driver.'

The little outburst stunned Brian into silence, and before he could think of something to say, a lorry came down the road towards them. 'Here comes the first job of the day,' Brian said, and walked off towards the truck.

It took them about half an hour to load the lorry. Brian was standing in the back; he would direct the driver to the appropriate pile of fittings and then Gator would throw them up one by one from the ground. Most of the fittings were small, U-shaped clay things, and Gator took great pleasure in throwing them as hard as possible at Brian in the lorry, like a rugby scrum-half feeding his fly-half. Brian caught them all, but Gator was using his strength to wear him out. When the lorry was full, both of them were sweating and Brian laughed. 'A nice little work-out?' he said.

'I was just warming up,' Gator replied.

The lorry drove round to the Portakabin and Ridley came out to hand over an invoice. Gator hadn't seen him all day and nodded at him.

For the rest of the morning, Gator went back to his pallet and read the *Sun*. He wasn't much interested in current affairs, but liked reading sensationalized news of crimes being committed up and down the country, to see if he could pick up any tips. Then at one o'clock Brian and Ridley came out and the three of them sauntered over to the canteen.

It was a few minutes' walk away, and was also used by the surrounding factories. At the serving area after grabbing a tray each they got a meal for only one pound fifty from the ladies behind the counter. Brian and Ridley had never made friends with the others, so they sat on a table by themselves. Gator made sure his plate was piled high, then went to join them.

'Did you hear that conversation Mr Carroll was having on the phone this morning?' Ridley was asking Brian as Gator arrived. Gator sat next to Ridley so Brian wouldn't get any ideas. Ridley was wearing a bow-tie again today, with the same brown tweed jacket he'd had on the day before. Gator guessed he was in his late fifties and he always looked worried.

'The one about planning permission?' asked Brian.

Ridley paused as he shovelled a forkful of cabbage and gravy into his mouth. When he'd swallowed, he said, 'I asked him about it when you were out loading that lorry. It seems Ellis Pipes didn't get planning permission to build our yard on that piece of land. I don't want to get you worried or anything, but I reckon they could close us down if that's the case.'

'You're joking,' Brian said.

'I asked Carroll about it. He said no, they hadn't got permission.'

'Then why did they build it?'

'Search me.'

Brian stroked his moustache, looked at Gator, and then went

95

back to his food. 'It's probably just red tape,' he said. 'They'll sort it out. They bloody better do. I gave up a bloody good job to come here.'

'Me too,' said Ridley, and they both looked at Gator.

'I didn't,' he said, and attacked his steak and kidney pie.

'Another thing I'm wary of,' Ridley continued. 'The far side of our yard is right on the edge of that slope going down into the valley. If we put too much stock on it, and we get a bit of rain, then I wouldn't be surprised if it all fell away.'

Brian laughed. 'You're a bit of a worrier, Ridley,' he said. 'That ground looks solid enough to me.'

'You mark my words,' Ridley said, emphasizing his point with a knife.

'I agree with Ridley,' Gator said. 'I was looking at that slope yesterday. It looks a bit sandy to me. Nothing solid.'

'Maybe that's the bit that held back the planning permission ' Ridley said.

Brian looked at them both and said, 'You're worrying about nothing. I'm sure it'll all be sorted out.'

Gator heaped a lump of mashed potato on to his fork and looked at Brian. 'Can we quote you on that?' he asked.

At five o'clock, at the end of the working day, Gator was walking down the rutted road towards the industrial estate's entrance when he saw Karl's Fiat bumping along towards him. The car stopped and the door flew open.

'Hop in,' said Karl, leaning over.

They drove out of Redgate and over to Orton to have another look at the post office. It was about a fifteen-minute drive, and the road was full of rush-hour traffic.

Orton was a small village situated near the M25. Like Woodvale, it was a place most people just passed through. It had one street of shops, including the post office which also served as the town's newsagent. Karl parked the Fiat down a side street and they walked into the shop.

Gator looked at some greetings cards while keeping an eye on the post-office counter which was protected by heavy-looking glass. Karl was over by the newspapers, flicking through magazines, also watching the counter. Eventually he bought a paper and motioned to Gator. They left and sat on a bench on the opposite side of the street.

'It's got to be a back-door job,' Gator said, stretching out on the bench, the skin on his back still burning from the day's sun. 'There're too many people coming and going to get in the front.'

'I agree,' Karl said.

'And the glass looks a bit too thick, as well. Even though it's an ancient post office. Always better to hit them at the back door.'

'I think you're right.'

'Let's go round and have a look.'

They left the bench, crossed the road again, and walked into a small car park. There was a six-foot wooden fence, over which were the shops' back yards.

'This is where to park the car,' Karl said. 'Nice and close.'

Gator nodded. 'We go over this fence when no one's looking, then we'll be out of sight as we try to get in the back.'

'Bash our way in?'

'We might have to. Might have to talk our way in. We'll ad lib.'

Karl looked worried. 'Ad lib is not a term I like to rely on.'

'I've done it before,' Gator said. 'Adds to the excitement.'

'Yeah, but you've also been banged up before. I don't want to get caught.'

'You're not chickening out, are you?'

'No. I just don't want to take any chances.'

Gator looked patiently at the ground. He had done just the one job with Karl, the petrol-station robbery, and Karl had only been driving the car for that one. Could he trust him to pull off something a little heavier? 'We did all right before, didn't we?' he said. 'That petrol station? We didn't have that all mapped out. It's the mark of a good criminal, the one that can make things up as he goes along, doesn't lose his nerve. It's all part of the challenge.'

'I suppose so,' Karl said.

'I know so,' Gator said.

They walked back to the Fiat in silence until Karl said, 'How much do you think they'll have in there?'

'I haven't got a clue, but it's more than I have at the moment.' Gator wasn't all that interested in the size of the score. To him it was the challenge, just something to do, to put a little excitement into his life. He could live for weeks off the thrill of knocking some place over, and he hadn't done anything criminal for over three months now. It was time to get started again. 'If it's all the same to you,' he said, 'I'd like to get on with it straight away. How about tomorrow?'

Karl looked at him with surprise. 'You'll be at work won't you?'

'We'll do it in my lunch hour,' Gator said. 'Come and pick me up at one o'clock.'

Karl started laughing. 'In your lunch hour. I like it. Are you what they call an habitual criminal?'

Gator had to laugh too. He liked the sound of that.

Back at Naughton Road, after dropping Gator off at his mother's, Karl made sure the Fiesta Azura was looking clean because a punter was coming round in the evening to look at it. Then he walked up the road for a Chinese takeaway and ate it in the living room, while the sound of Jason playing came from the basement below. That Jason, he was one dedicated fellow.

Eventually the punter turned up, and Karl was on his best smiling behaviour, pointing out all the good points, ignoring the few bad ones. Thirty minutes later, he had a pocketful of notes and was handing over the log book to the satisfied customer. He saluted from the pavement as the Azura pulled away.

When he walked back in the house Jason was standing in the living room.

'A successful sale?' he asked.

Karl reached in his pocket, pulled out the money, and flicked it in the air. 'My first since moving here,' he said. 'A two hundred-pound profit. Let's celebrate.'

'Not another party. I don't think my body can handle it.'

'Let's rent a video,' Karl said. 'Have a few drinks.'

'OK,' Jason said.

Jason followed Karl's example, and went up the road for a Chinese takeaway, while Karl drove the Fiat to the video shop. By the time he'd come back, Jason was sitting in the living room with his meal, a chilled bottle of white wine on the floor next to him, a leftover from the party. Jason had moved his TV and video back into the room. He dreaded to think what video Karl had rented. He was expecting a Jean-Claude Van Damme or Steven Seagal, but when he walked back in with a film called *Golden Balls* he was pleasantly surprised. 'Do you know what you've rented there Karl?' he asked.

'If it's called *Golden Balls*,' Karl said, 'then there must be loads of sex, and that's all right with me.'

'It's an arty Spanish film, you know,' Jason said. 'It's made by the same guy who directed *Jamon, Jamon*.'

'Come again?'

'He also did a film called *The Tit and the Moon*.'

Karl looked at the back cover of the video. 'Yeah, it mentions that here. I found it in the porno section.'

'Well it must have been put in the wrong place. That's an arty-farty subtitled film you've got there.'

'Shit.'

'But there's probably loads of sex. There was in *Jamon, Jamon*.'

'Who the fuck's Jamon? Is that Spanish for Eamonn?'

'Who gives a damn?'

'Certainly not me.'

'Get a drink and put the thing on.'

'OK. Here we go.' Karl slotted in the video.

*

At first Karl had problems reading the subtitles. How were you supposed to watch the picture and read something at the bottom at the same time? Hell, he may as well just be sitting reading a book, a pastime that never held any attraction for him. But as the film went on, and as the sex scenes started holding his attention, he thought that maybe a subtitled film wasn't such a bad thing after all. And the women in it were stunners. There was a particular one whom he recognized; she had dark hair. He asked Jason who she was.

'She was in *Pulp Fiction*,' Jason said. 'She played Bruce Willis's girlfriend.'

'Yeah, now I remember.'

'She's called Maria de Something.'

'Maria de Gorgeous Tits?'

Jason looked at him and they both laughed.

Karl was working his way through a bottle of red, and towards the end of the film his mind started drifting towards tomorrow's robbery. Why the fuck was he getting involved in such a thing again? He had just made an easy two hundred selling a car, and he could do the same again tomorrow. Why did he bother risking his freedom with that crazy fucker Gator? Was it to prove himself to Gator, to show that he could be a hardass too? To Gator it just came naturally, but Karl had to work at it. After the job tomorrow he would seriously consider not doing it ever again, just concentrate on what he was good at, which was selling cars. And, horror of horrors, maybe even go legal, start paying a bit of tax on what he earned. After all, he was getting on a bit now, and at twenty-four he'd have to start thinking more seriously about the future.

When the film finally finished Jason raised his glass at him.

'An excellent choice,' he said. 'Did you enjoy it?'

'I have to admit I did,' Karl said. 'It's good to see something where you have to use your brain a bit.'

'That's right,' Jason said. 'Much more rewarding.'

Karl finished off his wine and wondered how rewarding tomorrow would be. Whatever happened, he decided, tomorrow would be the last time he ever went on a job with Gator. Or with anyone else for that matter.

12

On Wednesday morning, Detective Sergeant Ian Kiddie was sitting in Jesse Morgan's office giving him the latest news on the Bosser household. The long and the short of it was that there wasn't any news. 'We've been sitting there for six days now and nothing's happened,' said Kiddie. 'We don't even know if Bosser's in the country. We don't know sod all.'

'Let's pack it in then,' Morgan said. 'I've got another idea, but I'll have to swing it with Cole first.'

'Oh yeah?'

'Wait here. I'll be back in a minute.'

Morgan walked out of the room and down the hall, and knocked on Superintendent Cole's door. Cole said come in, and Morgan entered and shut the door behind him. He sat down opposite Cole and outlined the situation for ten minutes. Cole was a born pen-pusher, a very neat man who looked anything but a policeman. Morgan had trouble understanding how he'd got this far, but it must be something to do with passing exams. He couldn't imagine Cole ever having any authority on the street. He was probably a few years younger than Morgan's forty-six, but looked about thirty: short fair hair, baby face. Looked like he didn't even have to shave every day. Cole could recognize a smart plan when he heard one, though, and he gave Morgan the go-ahead with his. Morgan thanked him and walked back down the hall to his office.

'Now here's what we do,' he said to Kiddie, not bothering to sit down. 'We release Stanley Bosser's body back to his wife, then pick up Bosser at the funeral. Simple.'

'Why didn't we think of that before?' Kiddie asked.

*

When lunchtime rolled around at one o'clock Phil Gator was waiting impatiently by the Portakabin for Karl to turn up. Brian and Ridley had already disappeared to the canteen. Gator had told them he had some errands to run, and might be back late. Brian had said that was OK. They weren't exactly rushed off their feet.

Gator could feel the butterflies in his stomach as he waited, which was always a good sign. He wished Karl would hurry up. Where was the silly fucker?

If he stood on tiptoe he could see Mr Carroll sitting behind his desk. What the old fart did all day was a mystery to him. In a way, Gator felt sorry for him. He obviously didn't have anything to live for except coming to work every day in this grotty yard. Gator knew that by the time he was that age he would have made enough not to have to work for anyone. Maybe he would have his own garage or some other little business, but he was damned sure he wouldn't be taking orders from anyone. Or maybe he would still be committing crimes. Would he ever get sick of doing them? He doubted it at the moment.

Then he saw Karl's Fiat coming up the road. Gator breathed a sigh of relief. When the car stopped next to him he climbed in and asked Karl why he was late.

'I forgot the sledgehammer,' Karl said. 'I was halfway here and had to turn back.'

'I hope you didn't forget anything else.'

'No. I double-checked.'

'You've got the guns?'

'Of course.'

'Good, I'm in the mood for action.'

For all his trepidation and the coaxing he needed before a job, Gator had to admit that Karl was pretty cool behind the wheel of a car. He drove them smoothly to Orton, not looking nervous at all. They went over the details of the robbery once again, and Gator felt confident, eager to get things under way.

They parked the Fiat in the small car park behind the post

office. They climbed out and opened the boot, slipped on thin pairs of gloves, then pulled out a crowbar, a sportsbag and the sledgehammer. They shut the boot, left the car doors unlocked and walked over to the back gate on the wooden fence.

'You going over first?' asked Karl.

'Wait a minute,' Gator said. He reached out and turned the knob on the gate; it swung open. 'Always worth a try,' he chuckled. They walked through the gate and inside.

'There's no challenge nowadays, is there?' Karl said, as he shut the gate behind them. They were in a small yard: a few dustbins, a bicycle, empty boxes. A low wire fence separated this yard from others on either side. Gator looked back over the wooden fence and noticed that the houses on the other side of the car park looked right over them. He nudged Karl.

'We'd better be quick,' he said. 'Some nosy fucker's bound to look out of one of those windows and see us.'

Karl turned around and said, 'Shit.' He turned to the back door of the post office and tried the knob. This one was locked.

The door didn't look too sturdy to Gator. He'd been through worse before. They got the crowbar and wedged it into the gap next to the lock. Karl held it horizontally in place while Gator picked up the sledgehammer and got ready to swing. 'When I hit it we're on our way,' he said. 'No turning back.'

'Let's go for it,' Karl said, and Gator was impressed again with how cool Karl was acting.

Gator stood with the sledgehammer at the ready, counted to three, and gave the crowbar an almighty whack. The crowbar lodged itself between the door and the frame. Gator dropped the sledgehammer on the ground and came round to Karl's side. They pushed on the crowbar together and the back door popped open.

'Fucking impressive,' Karl said. He opened the sportsbag and took out two woollen ski masks and two guns. He handed the .22 Colt to Gator and kept the .38 Smith and Wesson for himself.

They pulled the masks over their faces and walked inside the post office.

There were two people waiting for them, a middle-aged lady and a teenage bloke, obviously alerted by the noise. They were inside a storeroom full of stationery and cardboard boxes and were about to say something when Karl waved his gun at them and motioned them to the side. Gator went to one of the two internal doors in the room and opened it. Karl saw through to the shop before Gator quietly closed the door and locked it. He went to the other door and gently turned the handle.

Peeking through the crack, Gator saw an old guy sitting at the desk serving someone. He waited for what seemed like an age until the customer had gone then said, 'Pssst.'

The old guy turned around and saw the .22 that Gator was poking through the crack. Gator watched to see if the guy tripped any alarms, but he was smart: he left his desk and came to the door.

Gator let the old guy into the storeroom and waved him in Karl's direction. Karl shepherded him beside the middle-aged woman and the teenager. Now came the hard part.

Karl pointed the gun at the old guy's head and said, 'While we're waiting for my friend, I want you to open the safe for me.'

The old guy was shaking like a leaf.

'Just relax,' Karl said. 'It'll be over soon, and then you can tell it all to the local paper.'

The old guy walked away from the other two hostages and headed for the safe.

Gator was on his hands and knees with the sportsbag, crawling along the floor behind the post-office counter. He had thought this part through in bed the previous night so he knew roughly what he was going to do. His heart was pounding like a hammer, but this was what he lived for, this was what he got off on.

When he was under the counter he started reaching in drawers and emptying the whole lot into the sportsbag. There were money drawers, change drawers, drawers containing documents. Karl had said jokingly beforehand to get some car tax stickers so he wouldn't have to tax any of his cars any more, and lo and behold Gator came across some stickers and tipped them in the bag. He almost burst out laughing, but he was trying to be as quiet as possible. He could hear customers in the shop on the other side of the glass, maybe five or ten feet away. When he felt he had spent enough time in there, he got ready to go back to the storeroom along the floor.

'Excuse me?'

Gator froze at the sound of a woman's voice coming from the counter above.

'Excuse me, young man.'

Gator had to think quickly. He couldn't stand up with the mask on his face. The woman would start screaming and that would raise hell. So he pulled off the mask and stood up. Facing him from the other side of the glass was a little old pensioner.

'You're new here,' she said to him with a smile. 'Can I have two first-class stamps, please?'

Gator felt like giving her two first-class thumps, but smiled innocently at the woman instead and said, 'I'm just the cleaner. I'll go and get the old guy.'

Then he picked up the sportsbag and went into the storeroom.

Karl had the three hostages lined up and was holding two small canvas bags full of money. When Gator came back through the door Karl noticed he didn't have on his mask. Gator didn't realize his mistake until Karl said, 'Mask!' Gator put it back on but it was already too late. The three hostages had all got a good look.

Gator handed over the sportsbag to Karl, who noticed Gator's hands were shaking. Karl put his two canvas bags and gun in the bigger bag and zipped it up.

'A slight hitch in there,' Gator said. 'Take everything to the car and get it pulled round. I'll just tie up these three and be out.'

'You need any help?'

'No. Just get going.'

Karl picked up the bag and walked out.

In the back yard he took off the woollen mask and was glad to get some air on his face. He was sweating badly but still felt calm. He picked up the crowbar and sledgehammer and walked through the gate.

He continued unhurriedly across the car park, but halfway across he heard a gunshot from the post office. He thought he must be imagining things, but then he heard two more shots. He said, 'Jesus Christ!' out loud and ran the rest of the way to the car.

Gator walked out of the post office and over to the wooden gate. He still had his mask on and didn't take it off until Karl had the Fiat out of the car park and moving along at a steady pace. When he removed the mask it was dripping wet, and so was the front of his T-shirt. He noticed a few spots of blood there too.

Karl was talking to him but Gator couldn't think of a thing to say. He couldn't really focus on anything that was going on around him: passing cars, passing houses, summer sun, the gun in his lap. He had a new sensation surging through him and felt superhuman, on another plane.

Eventually he heard Karl saying, 'Speak to me, goddammit!'

Gator looked over at his friend and forced a smile. 'I think I just scored a hat-trick,' he said.

13

Karl had to drive Gator back to the house in Naughton Road to change his T-shirt. Gator insisted on going back to work, to make everything look normal, but he couldn't with those blood spots on him. On the drive back Karl tried talking to him but Gator was in a world of his own. Karl was wishing he was in a world of his own, too, like on a desert island somewhere, a thousand miles away from the nutter sitting next to him. What the hell had inspired him to shoot three innocent people?

Back at the house, Karl led Gator up to his bedroom. He found him a shirt of the same blue as the one he was wearing and watched while Gator changed. Then they walked back to the car, and Karl drove him into Redgate and over to the Holmethorpe Industrial Estate.

'I'll get rid of the .22,' Gator said during the drive.

'What about the other gun?' Karl asked.

'No need. That would just be a waste.'

Karl felt like saying something else about waste. Like three lives that had just gone down the drain. How did that rate on Gator's scale of waste?

As Karl was dropping Gator off a safe distance from the Portakabin he looked at his watch and saw they'd only been away one and a half hours. He mentioned the time to Gator, then added sarcastically, 'Not bad for a robbery and a triple murder.'

Gator didn't say a word. He just got out and walked away.

As he neared the Portakabin, Gator saw a truck in the yard with Brian in the back stacking fittings. Ridley was on the ground in shirtsleeves throwing up the fittings. Gator jogged back into the yard and over to where they were. He apologized to Brian and took over from Ridley who stayed to watch, sweating away in his office clothes.

When the truck was gone and Ridley was back in the office, Brian walked over to Gator. 'A good lunch hour?' he asked.

'I told you I might be late back,' Gator said.

'That's all right. I wasn't expecting that lorry to turn up anyway. Mr Carroll wanted to know where you were, though.'

'So you covered for me, right?'

'I covered for you.'

'Good man.'

'But now he's got another shit job for us to do.'

'Well, that's what I'm here for. I get a little bored lying out in the sun.'

'OK. Follow me.'

They spent the rest of the afternoon carrying various fittings backwards and forwards across the yard. It was all futile work as far as Gator was concerned, but it helped to keep him occupied, helped to keep his mind off things.

But he also knew that he'd just jumped way up the ladder on the criminal social scale, and towards the end of the day he couldn't help but walk with a little swagger in his step. Jesus fucking Christ! he was thinking. Someone might even write a book about me!

Frankie Bosser was in his hotel room, whiling away a long afternoon. He was sitting by the open window with a book on his lap, looking down on the main road at passers-by, seeing if he could recognize any of them. A few of the pensioners looked familiar, the kind of people that no one knows much about, always just there, going about their business in their sad little ways until one day they disappear. Frankie thought that maybe the people of Courmayeur would be thinking the same about him in a few years' time: there goes the poor Englishman who's not

109

allowed to return to his home country so he hides away in our town and makes out that he's happy. What a negative train of thought!

Frankie was also thinking of his little visit to Jason's the other day. He had listened to Jason sing for about an hour, and was baffled as to why he had never made it as a singer. Jason had told him that friends always thought he was talented because they never expected him to be any good. But if he put himself up against professional singers he was not in their class. Frankie still thought he was great, though, and told him so. What Jason needed was a manager and someone to put some faith and money behind him to get his career moving. But there was no way Frankie could make that sort of thing happen. He would be moving on in a few days.

He was diverted from his thoughts by the telephone ringing. He left the window and went to pick it up. It was Daniela.

'Some good news, Frankie,' she said. 'They're going to release your father's body and let us get on with the funeral.'

'That's great,' Frankie said. 'But why the sudden change of mind?'

'According to the doctor, the police say there's little chance of catching whoever hit Stanley. It happened over a week ago and they have no leads. They said if we want to bury him, then we can.'

'It seems like the best idea,' Frankie said. 'I don't think they're going to catch the guy. Do you need any help with the arrangements?'

'No. I think you'd still better stay out of sight.'

'Don't worry, I will.'

After hanging up, Frankie's main emotion was relief. He could finally bury his father and then go back to Italy. He was getting bored out of his skull hanging out in his room, although he was now on his third Elmore Leonard, this one called *Swag*. It was about a couple of criminals carrying out amusing robberies, living in a condo and pulling women. It made the criminal life seem very attractive, and Frankie wondered if that was a good thing to show in a book. But, then again, the criminal kind would probably never read this kind of book anyway. Or would they? And wasn't Frankie the criminal kind? No. He didn't think so.

Frankie's only worry now was why the police had changed their minds about the burial. Were they trying to set him up, waiting for him to put in an appearance at the funeral before arresting him? He had the feeling they were planning something. He thought he'd better just say goodbye to his father at the funeral home when the body was returned there, then let Daniela take care of the burial. He would sneak out of the country while the police were at the funeral looking for him.

Karl spent the afternoon alone in his room getting drunk. It took a whole bottle of wine to calm him down, and half of another one to relax him a bit more. He had the radio tuned to the local station and listened to the news each time it came around. The robbery was the main item, of course, a triple-murder in this part of the country being about as rare as Spurs winning the League. He listened to the policemen being interviewed. One was a guy called Cole, and the other was someone called Mulligan. They had a few lines of inquiry, they said, but weren't saying what they were. An incident room had been set up in a school in Orton. Karl was in half a mind just to make a run for it, jump on a ferry to Europe like Gator had done three months before. But he didn't like travelling, and had no desire to go to Europe. He wanted to stay in this new home of his and make a living selling cars. Why the hell should he run? It was Gator who had made all the trouble. He should be the one doing the running.

The money from the robbery totalled just over three thousand pounds, plus a load of forms and paperwork Gator had nicked, including some tax discs which were useless without the post-office stamp on them. Karl supposed that without the murders he would be quite pleased with this haul, but the killings put everything else in the shade. It could be a million pounds sitting in the bag under his bed, it wouldn't make any difference. He wanted to see Gator again soon, make him explain exactly what had happened.

He didn't have long to wait.

Just after six o'clock the front doorbell rang. Karl looked out of the window expecting to see police cars. There was nothing there. He walked downstairs and recognized Gator through the glass.

'What the fuck are you doing here?' asked Karl, ushering him in quietly.

'I need somewhere to stay,' Gator said.

'Well, you're not staying here,' Karl said, feeling a bit dizzy from the wine.

'I am staying here, end of story,' Gator said. 'Is the guitar man in?'

Karl pointed to a note on the hall table by the telephone. 'He's got a gig in London.'

Gator said, 'Good,' and relaxed a little. 'Look. You've got a spare room upstairs. I can kip in there and we'll give Jason the bad news when he comes home. We can slip him some extra money. We'll just say I got thrown out by my mum or something.'

'But why don't you just go home?'

'Because the cops'll go looking for the usual suspects and my name is bound to come up. I've done time, remember. They'll be round to see me tonight or tomorrow.'

'You should've thought of that before you blew three people away. I still can't believe it. I still can't fucking believe it!'

'Are you drunk?'

'Too fucking right I am!'

'Good. Lead me to the booze. I want to get there too.'

'I want a few fucking answers first.'

'OK. I'll explain it all in a minute.'

They went into the kitchen and Karl pulled a beer from the fridge. Gator reached for an open bottle of whisky that was on the counter, and drank straight from the bottle. He popped the can of beer and took a swig, then went back and forth between it and the whisky while Karl watched. He could see Gator starting to relax, like a tightly coiled spring unwinding. When he thought Gator was relaxed enough he said, 'Now tell me what the hell happened.'

They took their drinks outside to the back patio and sat on a couple of deckchairs. The sun was still in the sky, going down behind the trees at the bottom of the garden. Gator felt mellow in this perfect setting. He wondered if this might be the last sunset he ever saw in freedom. 'I panicked,' he told Karl. He watched Karl nodding, waiting for him to say more. 'I had to take my mask off in the post office,' he continued. 'I was just about to get out of there when this little old lady on the other side of the glass asks me for some stamps. What the fuck could I do? If I stood up with the mask on she would've screamed and blown the whole thing. So I took the mask off and stood up and told her I was just the cleaner. I said I'd go and get the old guy.'

'Well, that part was pretty cool,' said Karl, with a wry smile.

Gator smiled too. He had thought it pretty cool at the time as well. 'I wasn't worried about the old lady seeing my face. Old people are never good with their descriptions. But then, when I walked into the back room, and the three of them saw my face, I just knew the game was over. I didn't have any choice. There was no way I wanted to go back to gaol. I panicked. I thought I had to kill them.'

'You didn't have to kill anyone,' Karl said. 'We could've taken our chances. We would've got a year or two if we'd been caught. Now we'll definitely be caught, and you'll go down for ever and I'll get a nice long stretch too.' He raised his glass. 'Thanks very much.'

'There's no need to be so pessimistic,' said Gator. 'We'll just lie low until the whole thing blows over.'

'The whole thing will never blow over!' said Karl angrily. 'Have you ever heard of a triple murder not being solved?'

Gator put his fingers to his lips. 'Don't let the neighbours hear you. Of course there are murders that don't get solved.'

'Pretty fucking rarely in my experience. This is meant to be the best police force in the world, remember.'

Gator laughed. 'That's a load of crap for a start.'

'Well, I hope you're right.'

'I know I'm right.'

'And now you're going to stay here until the cops forget about you?'

'That's right.'

'That's your master plan?'

'That's right.'

'We'd better give Jason a load of money to keep him sweet.'

'That's exactly what we'll do. We'll pay him with the stolen money. How much did we get anyway?'

'Just over three thousand.'

'Good work. Good work.'

But Karl was giving him a dirty look so Gator looked seriously into his drink. He would have to keep a close eye on Karl to make sure he didn't do anything stupid. And keep a close eye on Jason, too, make sure he didn't drop them in it. Otherwise things could turn awkward, but he was quite confident at the moment that things would work out OK.

14

The next morning Jason woke up early, despite having tumbled into bed at about 1.30 a.m. He had played a gig in the West End of London, a small trendy club where he had topped the bill, the kind of place where beer only comes in a bottle, and the audience is there to watch each other rather than the music. He had played a forty-minute solo set, and been paid thirty pounds. When he subtracted the cost of petrol for the trip, the whole deal was hardly worth it. Why did he bother playing such places any more? Did he still harbour the faint hope of being discovered and offered a recording or songwriting deal? Was it the attention he liked, the looks he got from women afterwards? Or did he still get a kick from singing in front of people? He didn't really know. He would have to sort out his priorities in the near future, maybe concentrate just on teaching, which was a lot less hassle, and rewarding in its own kind of way. After all, he was now getting rent money from Karl. Did he really need to drive to London so regularly?

He decided to get up, even though it was only seven-thirty.

He went into the kitchen and put on the kettle. There were a lot of empties lying around on the counter. Karl must've had someone around last night for drinks.

His lodger didn't seem to be working out so bad after all. After his early misgivings Jason found himself actually starting to like the guy. He had enjoyed watching *Golden Balls* with him. That had been a laugh. It was the first time in a long while that he had watched a film with someone who wasn't Heather and it had made a refreshing change. Heather had always made noises when watching movies: little sighs and remarks, actually talking to the characters, and plenty of tears at the emotional bits. It had driven Jason to distraction when they'd watched a film in a cinema together. Not so embarrassing at home, but still distracting. Jason had been pleased to find that Karl watched mainly in silence, just a few dirty remarks about the women now and then. He had been quite amusing. Perhaps a bit of male bonding was what Jason needed at the moment. Christ, he hated that term! He got some bread out of the fridge and popped it in the toaster.

Jesse Morgan was woken up by his alarm after snatching an ineffectual three hours' sleep. Since the post-office triple murder every available policeman at the station, plus more from surrounding areas, had been congregating in the incident room in Orton. Then they had been running around like madmen looking for any leads, and it wouldn't stop until the killers had been caught. That the raid had been undertaken by two men who'd driven a red Fiat was about the only thing the police knew so far, but Morgan was confident the killers would be found. Something as messy as this would have to leave a trail somewhere.

Struggling to the side of his bed, Morgan picked up the phone and rang Nicola. This would be the only chance today he'd have to speak to her. She answered with a sleepy 'Hello?' after three rings.

'Did I wake you?' he asked.

'What time is it?'

'Just after seven-thirty.'

'You did then.'

'Sorry. It's the only time I can ring you. Did you hear about the triple murder yesterday?'

'No. I didn't hear any news yesterday. Hang on. Let me sit upright.'

He listened as she rustled into a more comfortable position. Funny how the word 'murder' got people's attention straight away. When she was ready he told her all about the post-office raid.

'I'm going to be working on this all hours until it's over,' he said. 'So if you don't hear from me, you'll know why.'

'Isn't that the classic policeman's line?'

'It's the classic break-up-a-relationship policeman's line. But I just want you to know that's not my intention here. I want to see you all the time at the moment. This couldn't have happened at a worse time.'

'You sweet-talker. Keep it up.'

He laughed. 'The truth is I can't get you out of my mind. I don't know if I'll be able to concentrate on the case.'

'Are you in charge of it?'

'No. When there's a big murder case in Woodvale they bring in outsiders to solve it. There are special murder squads surrounding the London area called the Area Major Investigation Pools. Or AMIP. When there's big trouble they come in and mop it up. They have more experience than us local bobbies. Supposedly.'

'But you used to work in London.'

'I know, but that counts for nothing. I'll be strictly doing donkey work on this one. They only trust us with domestic murders, the ones that are easy to solve.'

'It sounds like a bad deal to me.'

'If they think it works, then all well and good. Whatever gets the job done.'

'So who's the hot-shot detective in charge? Maybe I should meet him as you're just a dogsbody.'

Morgan chuckled. 'He's a guy called Mulligan. Been around for years. A good man. More murder experience than me. His bagman is called Mills.'

'What's a bagman?'

'His number two. Every detective has a number two. Are you sure you want to talk about this at seven-thirty in the morning?'

'It's quite interesting, really.'

'Not if you've done it for twenty years.'

'I haven't.'

'Maybe you should sign up.'

'I don't like the sight of blood.'

'Me neither.'

'So when am I going to see you?'

'Could be a few days. A week. I could drop in some time, but it'll only be a quick visit.'

'Dropping in for a quickie?'

'Sounds good to me.'

'I'll be waiting.'

He put the phone down a few minutes later, now wide awake and in a good mood. He walked naked to the bathroom and stood under a hot shower. It took his mind back to last Sunday. After relieving himself in the shower he had gone to the kitchen in his tracksuit to join Nicola for breakfast. She had cooked him a big plate of bacon, eggs, mushrooms and tomatoes. He wolfed that down in a few minutes while she watched in disbelief. He always felt hungry after running.

After breakfast they sat in the main room and read the *Mail on Sunday* together. She asked him questions about politics that he could only answer in the broadest terms. He found the subject extremely boring but if she wanted to talk about it in the future he would have to start taking an interest. He pointed out a few sports stories to her and was surprised to find she knew quite a bit about it. A woman who knew about sport? Now there was a rarity.

In the afternoon they'd gone for a walk in Woodvale Priory and then lay in the sun, talking non-stop. Morgan had never found it so easy talking to a woman before. He could pick any subject, and Nicola would always have a point of view, always be enthusiastic, constantly interested in his opinion. It was rare to find someone with whom the conversation just went back and forth so easily. Usually it was just one person holding forth while the other listened – Ian Kiddie sprang to mind – and then the other person would take over for a while. This fifty-fifty conversation was something to treasure. It had been an age since he'd talked to any person at length who wasn't a cop, and he was surprised to find that he could still do it. He was quite pleased with himself. But he would have to work at it, find new subjects to keep her amused.

Morgan had been married briefly a long time ago when in his twenties. It had seemed like a good idea at the time, but had dissolved after only a year. A few years later they divorced. Since then he had always lived alone, and no single relationship had lasted longer than six months. It was hard to make things work if you were a policeman, and he wondered if this one with Nicola would survive past the usual half-year. Maybe he would have to start changing his priorities; think about retiring if it got serious. He could do with a new direction in his life and perhaps this was the chance he'd been waiting for. He would have to see.

Their Sunday together had ended in the late afternoon with their first kiss, standing in the doorway of Nicola's flat. Because he hadn't kissed anyone for so long, Morgan had found the experience extremely erotic, but had also been pleased to find his technique hadn't deserted him. He was slightly more worried about the prospect of eventually climbing into bed with her. Would he remember what to do? Would he make a complete fool of himself? He would soon find out.

He stepped out of the shower, dried quickly and got dressed in his usual black trousers, white shirt, nondescript tie and drab sportscoat. Then he dried his hair with a blow-drier, and was walking to his car by eight-fifteen.

His job for today would be to go round addresses of known criminals in the area, seeing what they were up to yesterday. He would take Kiddie along with him and it would be a long day. But he could possibly drop in on Nicola in the Red Lion later.

There were voices coming from upstairs and the sound of two pairs of feet. Jason was down in the basement, still in his dressing gown, working over some lyrics for a new song. He was wonder-

119

ing which girl Karl had brought home last night, until he realized the second voice belonged to a man. He put down his songwriting book and walked up the stairs to have a look.

He found them in the living room, Karl and that scary guy called Gator, the one he'd met at the party and who had been round once or twice since. Both of them were drinking cups of tea, and both were sitting in their boxer shorts, enough muscle on show to make even Frank Bruno uneasy. Jason said good morning to them, and was about to leave when Karl waved him back in.

'Come and sit down,' Karl said. 'We've got something we need to ask you.'

Jason felt a little warning sign as he sat on the sofa next to Gator. Karl spoke from his armchair.

'We've got a little problem with Phil here. He's just been thrown out of his mum's house because she caught him with Wendy there last night. You remember Wendy. He was wondering if he could stay here for a few nights. You've got that other small room upstairs. Phil slept there last night, by the way.'

'I'll pay you by the day,' Gator said. 'Just name your price.'

'Just a few days?' Jason asked.

'Shouldn't be any longer,' Gator said. 'A week at the most. Just until I find somewhere else to live. I've got a job now so there shouldn't be any problem finding somewhere.'

Jason sat and thought about it, but what could he say with these two looking at him? He felt a little annoyed with Karl for putting him in such a position, but that small room was available, he only used it for some of his junk. And some more money would always come in handy. He seemed to be having money thrown at him these days, and it was a position he had to admit he enjoyed. Who wouldn't?

'OK,' he said. 'I don't see any problem. As long as it doesn't interfere with my lessons.'

'I'll be as quiet as a mouse,' Gator said. 'Thanks a lot.'

He held out a big hand and Jason reluctantly reached across to shake it. He could still remember Gator's iron grip from the last time he'd experienced it.

With Ian Kiddie at his side Jesse Morgan spent the whole day working his way down a computer printout of known felons in the Woodvale/Redgate area. He was surprised there were so many in such a so-called respectable area. The place obviously carried more secrets than even he would have thought imaginable. Most of the offences were fairly minor, though. Breaking and entering, GBH, drunk and disorderly, creating a nuisance. There weren't any armed robbers or mass murderers listed but, then again, he knew that most criminals were ambitious, and smaller crimes always led to bigger ones if you were a career criminal. It was all down to that thing called greed, and all criminals without exception had it. So every name on the list was worth checking. It was a tedious method of elimination but it had to be done.

After making it sweet with Jason, slipping him fifty quid for the spare bedroom, Gator went into the hall and made two telephone calls. First he phoned his mother at the swimming pool and told her that if the cops came looking for him, to tell them that he was still in Europe. She made the usual moans about, You're not in trouble again are you, Phil? and he placated her with his usual lies and reassurances. His mother was not a great fan of the police anyway, a grudge she had held for years, ever since she was caught and received a hefty fine for drinking and driving when she was in her late thirties. If she could help her only son put one over on them, then all well and good, and why should she worry? Gator didn't tell her where he was staying, but said he would make it up to her in a week or so. And he would, too. He'd buy her a nice present out of the stolen money.

The next call was to Brian at work. He told him he would be a little late as he was feeling a bit rough. Brian said not to worry about it; there was nothing much happening anyway. Gator promised to be in after lunch and Brian said, see you later. Gator smiled when he put down the phone. It was amazing how simple it was to manipulate people. Tell them a lie and they just want to believe it. Lies were sometimes easier to believe than the truth.

Next he found Karl, who was cleaning the Fiat in the garage. He was sitting in the front seat with a bucket of hot water in his lap and a rag in his hand.

'Getting rid of evidence?' Gator teased, leaning on the open door, looking down.

'Just checking,' Karl said, without looking at him. 'Do you think we should get rid of the crowbar and sledgehammer?'

'Maybe the crowbar,' Gator said. 'Might have some paint on it from the doorjamb. Sledgehammer's OK though. Lots of people have those.'

'The crowbar goes then,' Karl said, now looking at him, but acting a little subdued. 'You got rid of your gun, I presume?'

'Of course I did. But I'm not going to tell you where.'

'I don't want to know.'

'I need to get some clothes,' Gator said. 'Can you take me back to my house?'

'You think it'll be safe?'

'Safe enough. There won't be anyone watching it. I'll be in and out in five minutes. You can just drop me then pick me up.'

'OK. And I'll get rid of the crowbar on the way back.'

'Now you're thinking.'

Gator went inside to get his house keys, and when he returned Karl was ready, sitting in the blue Nissan with the engine running, the Fiat hidden away behind the closed garage doors.

Karl was beginning to feel depressed, as low as he'd felt in a long time, and the last person he wanted sitting next to him right now was Phil Gator. He sat in silence as they drove over to Gator's mother's house, and just grunted when Gator tried speaking to him.

When they arrived Gator told him to drive on a little. He was looking up and down the street, watching out for cops or anything else unusual. Then he told Karl to turn around.

'Drop me fifty yards away,' Gator said. 'Then come back in about five minutes.'

Karl drove around Woodvale, got caught up in the one-way system, and didn't get back to the house until ten minutes later.

'Where the fuck have you been?' asked Gator as he climbed back in, rucksack in hand.

'Traffic problems,' Karl said. 'Where to now?'

'Can you drop me at work and then take my rucksack back to the house?'

'Your wish is my command.'

'There's no need to get stroppy.'

'I think I'm entitled to a little strop.'

'You're like a fucking old woman.'

'Old women don't fuck,' Karl said. And he laughed.

'Now you're loosening up,' said Gator.

15

When Karl dropped Gator off at work it was just after two o'clock. Just as Gator was about to get out of the car Brian and Ridley came out of the canteen and headed back to the yard.

'There's my boss,' Gator said to Karl. 'The one with the moustache. The other guy works in the office.'

Karl watched the two men walking away from them, one tall guy and one short one. 'Did they say anything when you got back late yesterday?'

'Not really. It's all very easy-going here. The cushiest job I've ever had. Except that Brian keeps giving me the eye.'

'What do you mean?'

'Looking at my muscles. I think he fancies me.'

Karl laughed. 'Is he married?'

'Yeah.'

'Maybe you've got it wrong, then.'

'I don't think so.'

'Well, smack him one.'

'I may have to. But I don't want to lose my job.'

Karl looked at Gator to see if he was being serious. 'You don't want to lose your job? I would say that's the least of your worries right now.'

Gator was staring at him. 'You worry too much. I'll see you later.' He stepped out of the car, shutting the door just a little too hard, and jogged to catch up with the other two.

Later in the afternoon Gator was sitting with Brian on a twelve-inch pipe that was lying on the ground in the yard. They were between two stacks of pipes so they were hidden from the office. Next to them was the wire fence and then the slope leading down into the quarry, the slope that had so worried Ridley. Gator agreed the ground looked sandy, and it would be interesting to see what would happen when a big thunderstorm came along. He glanced at the clear blue sky and thought there wasn't much chance of that for a while. It hadn't rained since the day he came back from Europe.

They had stopped for an orange-juice break, Brian sharing his flask and munching on a sandwich from his lunch box. They had just spent the previous two hours shifting more stacks of pipes around, rearranging the yard yet again for the perfectionist Mr Carroll.

Brian said, 'You'd better keep a clean nose for the next few weeks. All this arriving late and long lunch breaks. Carroll is thinking of getting someone else already.'

'Yeah?' Gator said. 'Well, it won't happen again. It was just a one-off thing.'

'Anything I can help with?'

Gator shook his head. 'I don't think so.' He handed the cup he was sharing back to Brian. As he passed it over Brian's hand brushed his and it was more than an accident, more like a lingering touch.

'Tell me,' Gator said. 'Am I just imagining it or do you fancy me?'

Brian smiled and poured some juice into the cup. 'You intrigue me,' he said.

'Intrigue? Well, that's the first time someone's told me that.'

'Can I ask you a personal question?' Brian said.

'If you like.'

Brian took a sip of juice and then turned around to straddle the pipe so he was facing Gator directly. 'Have you ever been in prison?'

Gator wasn't prepared for that one so he hesitated before answering. He contemplated lying but then thought, To hell with it. What difference would it make? 'Yeah, I have,' he said. 'Six months, a few years ago.'

Brian half punched the air. 'I knew it!' he said. 'I knew it!'

'What're you so excited about?' asked Gator.

'Nothing. I just had a hunch, that's all. You just struck me as someone who might've done time. Although I looked at the forms you filled in, and there was no mention of it there.'

'It's not something you want to tell the world about.'

'I suppose not. So what did you do?'

Gator smiled. 'I was somewhat naive at the time. I held up a building society in Croydon with a fake gun. Got out of there with the money as well, but then ran out of the door into the waiting arms of a copper. Just bad luck, really.'

'Shit.'

'I felt like a fucking idiot.'

'I bet you did.'

'So they sentenced me to a year. First offence. I did six months and then got out of there. Six months of boredom.'

'In what way?'

'Routine. You're tied to the same old thing every day. It becomes engraved in your mind.'

'So what is the routine?'

Gator cast his mind back three years; it wasn't something he was likely to forget. 'You get up at a quarter to seven, slop out, have a wash and then go for breakfast. Where I was there was no canteen so we used to eat our meals locked up in our cells. It was just me and one other bloke. Then from eight till eleven we went to work on whatever little job they had for us that week. Mostly I did cleaning. I scrubbed enough floors to last three lifetimes. When I get my own house some time down the line I'm going to get me a woman to do all that. I can't stand fucking cleaning.'

'Me neither.' Brian laughed.

'Then lunch was at eleven-twenty and we were locked in our cells until one o'clock. Then from one till two, the only bearable bit of the day, an hour in the gym. When I got out of there I was as fit as fucking Superman.'

'You told me you didn't work out.'

'Well, I don't. I only did it in there. If I did it out here it would remind me of prison.'

'Fair enough. What was next on the agenda?'

'After two we went back to work, and then were in our cells by four. High tea was served at four-twenty and we were locked up again until six.'

'Blimey,' Brian said. 'What did you do locked up all that time?'

'Lie on my bunk and look at the ceiling most of the time. I had a radio, so we used to listen to that. I can't stand reading. Except for newspapers.'

'What was the other bloke in your cell like?'

'He was OK. A bit younger than me.' Gator didn't want to talk about Teddy. They had fucked each other ragged for most of the six months. 'Then, after six,' he continued, 'we had what they used to call "association". We were allowed to watch TV, play snooker or table tennis, listen to music or, if you were a real goody two-shoes, take classes in the education unit. Then at eight it was back to your cell for supper, and, bang, the door was shut for the rest of the night.'

'A long time to be locked up.'

'It sure was. I used to go to bed earlier than when I was a kid.'

'What happened if you needed a shit in the middle of the night? Did they let you out?'

'You must be joking. You had to do it in the slop bucket, but then you'd have the stink in the cell all night. Your cellmate wouldn't think much of that idea. So we used to do it in newspaper and then throw it out of the window. Another of my jobs was picking up the balls of newspaper in the mornings. A delightful way to live, don't you think?'

Brian was screwing up his face. 'It's barbaric.'

'You wouldn't think these things would still happen would you?'

'Most people don't know about it.'

'Most people don't want to know about it.'

They were silent for a while but Gator felt the conversation wasn't over yet. He looked out into the quarry. On the other side of the hill was the skeleton of the old Fuller's Earth factory. Gator had never worked there but knew a few blokes who had. He'd heard it was dirty work, digging up clay which was then dried out and bagged up as dust, which was used mainly for refining oils.

'What about sex?' Brian asked. 'Did you ever see any of that going on?'

Gator chuckled. That was usually one of the first questions people asked about prison life. Especially blokes. He was surprised it had taken Brian so long. To most men the thought of having a dick up their bum was the worst thing imaginable. Gator knew that there was much worse though: like being beaten up or knifed. And he had seen plenty of that. He looked at Brian and said, 'Sure, I saw some.'

Now Brian was getting really interested. 'Did you ever do it yourself?' he asked.

Gator hesitated. Why should he tell Brian all his secrets? All those nights with Teddy, getting it on. What did it have to do with him? But before he knew it he was saying, 'Sure I did.'

Brian smiled. 'What was it like?'

Gator paused again. He had never told a bloke outside of prison about what he did inside. Not even Karl. But he suspected Karl knew a bit about what had gone on, and that would explain his reaction when he'd woken up last Sunday to find Gator in his bed. But Gator didn't have any designs on Karl, it had just been somewhere to sleep. And besides, he had never fucked a man anywhere but in prison. He had always managed to get women on the outside, so why would he want a man?

'You really want to know?' Gator asked.

'Yeah,' Brian said.

Gator took a deep breath. 'Well, at first it's really painful. If you get some bastard who's not too careful you'll have a sore arse for over a week and a lot of bleeding. The best way is with a lot of lubrication. I would recommend KY jelly. After a while, though, your arse starts to loosen up and things become easier. It's not such a bad feeling, really.'

'Wow!'

'But it's a whole lot better fucking someone up the arse than the other way round. Fucking an arse can be a really pleasurable experience. It's tighter than a woman so you get more friction, and your orgasm is more intense. In fact, I would say my most memorable orgasms have been up someone's arse.'

'But you go out with women, right?'

'Yeah. I wouldn't want to go out with a man on the outside. Women are more fun. They're more entertaining to talk to. I would only fuck a man in prison. The perfect world, of course, is a woman who likes taking it up the arse. But they're quite hard to find.'

'They're probably quite scared by it.'

'Most people are.'

They fell into another silence. Brian was looking at Gator with renewed respect.

'Why are you so interested, anyway?' Gator asked. 'Not getting enough at home?'

'That's partly it,' Brian said. 'Seeing as how you're being so honest I may as well tell you the whole story.'

'Please do. There doesn't seem to be much else going on.'

Brian scratched his head with embarrassment, and then stroked his moustache. He was delaying the moment of truth. 'Well, you see, I was married when I was twenty-two, and I'd only slept with one woman before I met Wendy.'

'Hey, snap!'

'Pardon?'

'My girl's called Wendy as well.'

'Does she take it up the arse?'

'No way.'

'Pity. Anyway, Wendy was twenty. We had sex pretty regularly to start with, but then came the first kid, when I was twenty-five, and the second, when I was twenty-seven. Wendy was always too tired after that, the kids keeping her up all hours, and I can honestly say that now we have sex about twice a year. Once on my birthday and once at Christmas.'

'You're joking.'

'I'm serious. Twice a year. OK, so the dates may vary, but twice a year is about all I get.'

'How old are you now?'

'Thirty-five.'

'That's bad luck.'

'And when we do have sex, she just lies there and doesn't do a thing.'

Gator laughed. He shook his head.

'I spend most of my time,' Brian continued, 'looking out of the window at girls walking down the street, tossing off to the sight of them. My favourite is my next-door neighbour. Now she's a tasty piece of stuff. In the summer she's out in the garden in a bikini, and I'm up in the bedroom beating my meat. That's about as close to a great orgasm as I get these days.'

'I've done that before myself,' said Gator.

'I'm glad I'm not the only one.'

'You and thousands of other men around the world. Just make sure no one sees you, though. You don't want to get done for exposing yourself.' Gator chuckled. 'There was this bloke in prison I was chatting to one day. He was fixated with his next-door neighbour as well. Used to toss off whenever he saw her. One day he was so frustrated for a sight of her he tossed off looking out of his window at her car.'

'You're pulling my leg.'

'I'm serious!'

'That's about as sad as it gets.'

'You're telling me.'

'So, anyway,' Brian said. 'The long and the short of it is, I'm dying for a decent fuck. I don't know any women that would

130

want to go out with me, so lately I've been thinking about men. Men have such a different attitude towards sex, such an animal attitude, and I think maybe that's what I need. I don't want anything emotional. I just need the physical side. Is that hard to understand?'

'I'm with you all the way,' Gator said. 'That's what most men need. It's the women who want all the emotional stuff. Men just want to fuck. That's why you see so many gay men these days. Cutting out all that emotional crap and just getting down to it. That's also why there are so many lesbians around as well. Women can only really relate to other women. It's all a bit fucked up really.'

'Exactly.'

Gator looked at his watch. 'Shouldn't we be getting back to work?'

Brian looked round the edge of the stack of pipes towards the office. 'No. Fuck 'em.' He turned back to Gator. 'It's making me a bit horny talking about all this sex. You wouldn't fancy having a go with me, would you? Just so I know what it's like.'

Gator grinned. He guessed it had been leading to this. Poor, frustrated Brian. But it was a long time since he'd had a piece of arse himself. It might be quite nice to try it again, out here in the summer sun. Break his golden rule about not fucking men outside of prison.

'OK,' he said. 'But I don't want any kissing. I'm not into any of that. Especially with that awful moustache of yours.'

'I don't fancy kissing you either.'

Gator nodded. 'But we need some lubrication. What can we use?'

Brian reached down for his lunch box. He snapped it open and took out two small tubs of margarine. 'I brought these along,' he said. 'It'll be nice and melted by now.'

'You've been planning this all along.'

'Ever since I first saw you,' Brian said. 'I always thought you'd be the first one.'

131

'You're not getting all emotional, are you?'

Brian laughed. He took a couple of condoms out of the lunch box too. 'I thought we'd better use these as well,' he said.

Gator stood up and stretched. 'All right,' he said. 'I'll do you first. Let's get to it.'

When it was all over, they were sitting back on the pipe again, both feeling a bit uneasy.

Brian said, 'My arse is burning. How about yours?'

'Mine's OK,' said Gator. 'Nice and warm, though. So how did you enjoy it?'

'It was good,' Brian said. 'A really intense orgasm.'

'I told you it would be. The trouble is, you'll want more now. And where will you get it?'

'Maybe I'll have to go into London. There are plenty of gay bars up there, aren't there?'

'They're everywhere you look. You'll be able to get laid regularly. Just be careful about it.'

'Do you ever go in them?'

'No. As I said before, I don't fuck men outside of prison. You're the first.'

Brian smiled. 'I'm honoured. How can I ever repay you?'

Gator grinned at him. 'Well, there is one small favour you could do me. And I'll let you fuck me again if you do it.'

'Just tell me what it is,' Brian said.

'Well, that lunch break when I came back late? If the cops ever come around asking questions, can you just tell them I was with you all the time, having lunch?'

'Like an alibi?'

'Yeah.'

'I thought you were up to something. Are you going to tell me what?'

'Of course not.'

Brian reached out and squeezed Gator's hand. 'Hey, no problem,' he said.

16

On Thursday evening Frankie Bosser left his hotel room and drove the rented Sierra over to Woodvale. He had been invited to Daniela's for supper, and as it appeared the cops had forgotten all about him for now he had decided to take the risk and go over for a meal. It was the first time he'd been there since his return.

It was a humid summer's evening, the earlier blue sky now a dark grey, but Frankie was still sweating freely even though he had the car windows down. His grey trousers were sticking to the car seat, his white shirt to his back and he wished he'd brought some shorts along for the trip. There wasn't any point in buying any now, though; yesterday he had booked his return flight to Italy for Monday morning. He would see his father's body at the funeral home tomorrow, lie low for the weekend, and then be gone. And not a moment too soon. He would be back in Italy on Monday afternoon, and that would mean he had been away for nearly two weeks. Two weeks in which he had done hardly anything but stay in his hotel room and read Elmore Leonard novels. Well, at least that discovery was one bonus of the trip.

He parked the car a few streets away from his father's house and walked the rest of the way. He came to the alley that led to the back garden and walked along it slowly. There were hedges on either side, and only enough room for one person to walk. Frankie looked through the hedges towards the big detached houses, each with a garden about fifty yards square. The thought of living somewhere like this one day was appealing, but would he ever be able to? Would he forever be living in a country where English was not the native tongue?

He rounded a curve in the alley and there was a man ahead, coming towards him with a golden Labrador. The man was tall with red hair and a moustache. Frankie's immediate reaction was cop, but then he thought, What would a cop be doing walking a dog along this alley at seven in the evening? Or maybe the dog was his cover? Frankie smiled at his own paranoia, and relaxed as the man came nearer.

'Evening,' the man said to him, as they squeezed past each other. Frankie had to step over the dog's lead and nearly got caught up in it. He returned a non-committal greeting.

'Looks like rain,' the man said as Frankie was about to walk on. A thick Scottish accent.

Frankie looked at the sky and said, 'You may be right.'

The man smiled and they caught each other's eye. Frankie nodded and moved on.

He came to the back of his father's house, flipped open the gate and walked inside. He examined the garden as he walked through: the lawn needing a cut, neat flower beds at the borders. The motorized mower was in the middle, looking a bit forlorn without its owner sitting on top. Frankie could remember when his father had first bought the machine, maybe ten years before. He had come round for Sunday lunch, and his father had been so proud of his new toy that he had sat on it for the hour the small group had spent enjoying their aperitifs. Then, much to everyone's amusement, his father had started up the mower and driven it right to the kitchen door, before dismounting and going inside to carve the meat. Frankie was in half a mind to do the same thing now: drive up to the house and surprise Daniela. She might find it too upsetting, though.

Frankie could see Daniela through the rear window, and he waved to her as he approached. Then she was at the back door to greet him, giving him a big hug and a kiss on both cheeks.

'I was just thinking about the mower,' Frankie said. 'You remember that time he drove it to the kitchen door?'

Daniela laughed, her eyes filling up with tears at the thought.

'Stanley was always a man for a joke. He always wanted people to laugh at him.'

Frankie saw a half-empty bottle of red wine on the table and was almost tempted to have a drink himself. He opted instead for a ginger ale, and sat at the kitchen table while Daniela carried on preparing the meal.

'Are you going to sell the house now?' Frankie asked, eating some peanuts from a dish.

'I'm putting it on the market next week,' Daniela said. 'Whether it'll sell, I don't know.'

'And then what?'

'If it sells, I might move back to Italy. Your father is what kept me here and now I have no ties. I miss Italy.'

'Me too,' said Frankie. 'But coming home brings a lot of memories back. I don't know which country I want to live in.'

'A little confused?'

'More than a little. When I'm in Italy I miss England nearly every day. Now I'm back here I think that I could be romanticizing about the place. But really I have no choice in the matter. I'll have to live in Italy.'

'Maybe I'll come and live near you. Then we can cheer each other up.'

'That would be nice,' Frankie said. He ate some more peanuts. 'So what time do I have to be at the funeral home tomorrow?'

'Eleven o'clock,' Daniela said. 'I'm not looking forward to it.'

'Me neither, but that's what I came over for. I have to say goodbye to him.'

Daniela took a sip of red wine. 'You're a good boy, Frankie. It's a shame it all turned out like this.'

'Life's full of surprises.' Frankie shrugged. 'Some good, some bad.'

Daniela nodded. 'Shall we eat?' she said.

From a telephone box about fifty yards away from the Bosser house, Detective Sergeant Ian Kiddie phoned the police station.

He asked for Jesse Morgan but was told he wasn't there, so instead got put through to Sergeant Wicks, a long-term Woodvale policeman, like himself. He told him he had just seen Frankie Bosser in the alley behind Stanley Bosser's house.

'What were you doing behind the Bosser house?' asked Wicks.

'Walking my dog,' Kiddie said. 'I only live a few miles away, you know.'

'Is that the dog without any spots?' Wicks asked.

'The very same.'

'Are you sure it was Bosser?'

'Positive. Listen,' he said, 'this isn't the time for twenty questions. I need two men and a car. Can you send them over right away? I'll pick Bosser up when he comes out.'

'I'll see who I can scrounge up. We're up to our oxters over here, though.'

'Very funny,' Kiddie said. 'Be as quick as you can. I don't know how long he'll be, and there are three possible exits.'

'OK. They'll be there in five minutes.'

'Good. I'm in the phone box in Raglan Road.'

'Righto.'

Kiddie stepped out of the phone box and knelt down beside Spotless, his Labrador. He patted him on the head and said, 'You're going to see some action tonight, my friend.' Spotless understood perfectly, jumped up, and started licking Kiddie's face.

They'd just finished eating when the rain came down, still sitting in the kitchen. It was about ten o'clock.

'Sounds like a heavy one,' Frankie said, after the first flash of lightning and subsequent rumble of thunder.

They stood at the window for a while and watched the rain run down the glass, the back garden illuminated by a light on the garage wall.

'Do you want the mower moved?' asked Frankie.

Daniela shook her head. 'I'll leave it with the house when I move. I won't need it where I'm going.'

Frankie looked at his father's machine and felt sad. The rain would seep its way under the hood and into the engine. It would probably be ruined. But, then again, these machines were so tough it might survive.

'I'm going to get soaked going home,' Frankie said. 'I parked a couple of streets away.'

'I'll drive you if you like,' said Daniela.

'You've been drinking.'

'Not too much. I'm used to it.'

'OK. That would be good.' Frankie turned away from the window. 'Do you remember what any of the policemen watching the house looked like?' he asked.

'What do you mean?'

'When I was walking down the back alley I passed a ginger-haired man with a dog. A Labrador. He had a ginger moustache as well. He looked like a cop to me, but maybe I'm just being paranoid.'

'The Labrador had a ginger moustache?' Daniela teased.

'You know what I mean. Does he sound familiar?'

'Not really. I only saw them from the window. I couldn't make out any faces. But if you're worried, maybe I'd better drive you all the way home.'

'That may be too risky. If they're still out there, they might follow us.'

'Why don't we go for a drive and see? You can lie down on the back seat.'

'Sounds good to me. Let's clear away the dishes first.'

'Leave those. I have all the time in the world at the moment. I'll do them tomorrow.'

When the police car arrived, Ian Kiddie took charge and sent the two disgruntled policemen on their way to watch either end of the alley. When the rain started coming down, Kiddie realized what a wise move that had been. He felt a bit sorry for the two men when it really started chucking it down, but it was all part of the job and he was their superior, so why shouldn't he be the one sitting nice and dry in the car? Besides, he still had Spotless with him. He couldn't leave him out in the rain, could he?

It was a little after ten o'clock when Kiddie saw the automatic garage door opening, with Daniela Bosser sitting inside her car, clearly silhouetted against the garage light. Kiddie watched the car drive out slowly and swerve round Stanley Bosser's white van that was still parked in the drive. The automatic garage doors shut behind her.

Kiddie turned the ignition key in the car. He was convinced that Frankie Bosser would be lying down on the back seat.

From the darkness of the living-room window Frankie watched the car going down the drive. He had changed his mind about lying down on the back seat, had thought it a bit melodramatic, like kids playing cops and robbers. The smarter thing to do would be to wait and see if anyone followed Daniela. That would tell him for sure either way. And it didn't take long for his worst suspicions to be confirmed.

He saw the unmarked police car pull away from the opposite kerb as soon as Daniela pulled on to the road. He couldn't make out the face in the front seat but could clearly see the one in the back. It was the face of a dog, the dog that had been in the alley. Frankie laughed. Man's best friend was certainly his at that moment.

He stepped away from the window, went into the hall, picked up a spare umbrella and walked out into the rain.

Phil Gator was listening to the rain, lying on his single bed in Jason's spare room, his heart pumping like a jackhammer, in spite of the whisky he'd consumed. He usually found the sound of rain comforting, but it would take more than that to calm his nerves at the moment. He was taking a day at a time and wondering what tomorrow would bring. He would go to work as normal and wonder, as he had done today, if every car heading towards the builders' yard was a cop car, and if some figure of doom would climb out of the vehicle and head towards him. And, some time tomorrow, he'd probably end up letting Brian fuck him again, to keep him sweet as his alibi. He hadn't particularly enjoyed their little scene today, but if that was what it took to be safe, then that was what he would have to do. It was all about survival now, and sometimes desperate measures had to be taken.

He turned over on his side and tried to will himself to sleep. But there was too much going on outside. A flash of lightning and then rolling thunder. Christ! It sounded like the world was coming to an end. And maybe it was. Maybe it was.

17

The next morning, Friday, Jesse Morgan picked up Ian Kiddie from his house, for another day of driving round and asking people questions they didn't want to answer. There were still no leads on the triple murder, and Cole and Mulligan were starting to get desperate. The longer a murder investigation dragged on, the harder it was to find the killer. All policemen knew that and it always added to the pressure they were under, as if they weren't under enough already. And Ian Kiddie looked under pressure now, as he walked down the drive from his house and climbed in the passenger's side. Morgan asked him what was wrong.

'Fucking Frankie Bosser, that's what.' Kiddie scowled.

'You're not still after him, are you? I thought you'd given up on that.'

'I never give up on anything, you should know that.'

Kiddie told him all about the previous night, seeing Bosser at his father's house and setting up a watch. Then following Daniela Bosser in her car.

'I was certain Bosser was in the back,' Kiddie continued. 'But all she did was drive to Redgate and then come home again. Got me away from the house for about fifteen minutes. And then I got it. Bosser would've seen me driving after her and then just walked out of the front door.'

'But how did he know the house was being watched?'

'The criminal's paranoia. Always on guard, always on the lookout. When I bumped into him in the alley he must've known I was a cop. It really pisses me off the way a criminal can always

140

tell who we are straight away. I mean, how do they do that? Is it really that obvious?'

Morgan looked across at Kiddie and laughed. 'It's your haircut. It's too severe. Try getting a little length in it.'

'Yours isn't exactly long.'

'I know. But just take that military look off it. My beard helps too, of course.'

'I've got a moustache, though,' said Kiddie defensively.

'Yeah, but moustaches make you look even more military. Or gay.'

'Cheers. Thanks a lot.'

Morgan smiled. 'Why don't you just post a man at the funeral home? He's bound to go there some time.'

'I've already done that. Got the time he's going to be there too.'

'There you are then. You've got it all sussed.'

Morgan tried concentrating on his driving. He was feeling in a good mood despite not getting enough sleep again last night. He had managed to see Nicola for half an hour in the Red Lion, and that was all he could think about. If he could just get a daily fix of her, it would help him through the long hours he would have to work until the end of the investigation. And then they could get down to the serious things, like maybe jumping naked between some sheets together. He found it ironic that after such a long time without sex he should now be sidetracked by the biggest murder hunt the area had seen for some twenty years. Still, he guessed he and Nicola would get there in the end. The thought of it gave him a stirring in his groin, so he forced himself to think of something else.

After last night's storm the streets looked a mess, branches and twigs scattered all over the place, water still lying in the gutters. The sun was out, though, and once the council got the streets swept, everything would return to normal.

Morgan pulled the car into the parking lot of Woodvale's swimming pool.

'Who have we got first,' asked Kiddie, 'or are we just going for a swim?'

141

'That Mrs Gator we tried to interview yesterday. I found out she works here. We'll see if she knows anything about her son's whereabouts.'

'Phil Gator?'

'Yeah. Hard man and sometime petty criminal.'

'Can't say I know him.'

'Me neither. But the computer does.'

They walked across the car park and through the swing doors at the entrance. The smell of chlorine hit Morgan immediately, and reminded him of unhappy schooldays and swimming classes. He hated swimming, and had never been any good at it.

The first person they talked to was Mrs Gator, the woman sitting behind the glass waiting to give them tickets and locker-room keys. Morgan guessed she was in her fifties, with a grey expression on her face and drably dressed in the same colour. She had curly grey hair too and the tired look of a woman who had given up long ago, who was just marking time until her ship came in. Morgan felt sorry for her straight away.

After they'd told her who they were, she picked up a telephone and got another member of staff to take over. Then she came out of the cubicle and led them down a hall to an office. The sound of screaming kids came from the pool.

Inside the office they formed a triangle with their chairs and sat down. Mrs Gator had her hands in her lap, stroking her fingers, looking more than a little nervous. For the next ten minutes she told them that she hadn't seen her son for months, that he had gone to Europe to travel but hadn't returned yet. They discovered a little about his criminal past, his stretch in prison three years before for robbery, and a few other scrapes, such as disturbing the peace and threatening behaviour. It was all rather fruitless, thought Morgan. Another member of the public who didn't want to tell them the truth. Another mother who wanted to protect her son. They had seen a few of those yesterday and today looked like being just as frustrating.

Outside, walking back to the car, Morgan said, 'Why do we

bother? What is the fucking point?' His earlier good mood had vanished.

'Because someone has to,' Kiddie said. 'If we didn't, who else would?'

'You're pretty optimistic for a Scot, aren't you?' said Morgan.

'Only when you're not,' replied Kiddie. 'That's why we make such a good team.'

Morgan had to agree with that. When one was down the other would drag him back up. But there had to come a time when he would just stay down, in spite of Kiddie's efforts.

When Phil Gator got to work that morning, he saw Old Man Carroll and Brian standing on the far side of the yard. Then, as he walked past the Portakabin, Ridley came rushing out looking like he was about to have a nervous breakdown. He marched up to Gator agitatedly, and without even a good morning said, 'I told you it would happen! I told you, I told Brian, I told Carroll, but did anyone listen?'

Gator stopped walking and said, 'What's up?'

Ridley pointed to the far side of the yard, to Brian and Carroll. 'Remember that dodgy piece of ground that the yard's built on? Remember we didn't get planning permission to be here? Remember all that sand?'

Gator nodded and looked over to where Ridley was pointing. Then he got the point. All the stock and the wire fence on the far side of the yard had disappeared. He hadn't noticed at first. 'You mean the storm has washed it all away?' he said.

'Too damned right. Washed away the stock and washed away my job. I told them all along! How can they build a yard without permission? They should've told me before I took the job. I would never have applied in the first place!'

But Gator had stopped listening to Ridley and was now wandering over towards Brian and Carroll. He heard Ridley following him.

'Stupid old bastard,' muttered Ridley. 'Why didn't he retire when he was meant to, like most old people do. Normal people can't wait to retire!'

The rest of the yard looked OK to Gator: just a few fittings that had toppled over. In fact, the rain had made all the pipes look sparkling clean.

Brian turned and smiled at Gator when he saw him, but Carroll didn't even acknowledge him. Gator thought maybe he'd have to retire the old bastard himself. He stood next to Brian and looked down at the mess below.

The storm had eroded about ten feet of the yard, about fifty yards in length, and all the pipes on that section of ground had toppled down the side, into the valley below. There were broken pipes everywhere, and a few that had survived.

Then Gator heard Carroll speaking in that stupid colonel's voice of his. 'We'll have to bring the unbroken pipes up, of course. Then put in an insurance claim.'

Ridley, standing next to Carroll, said, 'How can it be insured? The insurers wouldn't have touched it.'

Carroll hadn't thought of that. 'It must be insured. I'll ring up head office and see.' He turned to Brian. 'If you could start bringing the unbroken ones up with Phil.' He seemed to notice Gator for the first time, but still didn't acknowledge him. 'I'll go and make some phone calls.' And then he was wandering off, head held high, his white moustache proudly displayed.

'What a prick,' Gator said. 'That's going to be a great job, that is.'

'Never mind,' Brian said. 'It'll keep us busy.'

'I'll give you a hand, if you like,' Ridley said.

'You'll only get covered in muck,' Brian said. 'Why don't you be our spy on the inside. Go and listen to Carroll's phone calls, and see if we're all about to lose our jobs.'

'That's a very good idea,' said Ridley and he trotted off to catch up with Carroll.

Gator and Brian looked down at the rubble below.

'Are you thinking what I'm thinking?' asked Brian.

'Probably not,' Gator said, 'but I'm sure you're about to tell me.'

Brian pointed at a stack of pipes below them. 'That stack over there,' he said. 'That's the one we fucked behind yesterday.'

Frankie Bosser made his way to the funeral home in his rented Sierra. He was dressed in a suit and tie for the occasion, even though it was far too hot for such formal wear. He was feeling a little nervous as he drove, apprehensive about seeing his father for the last time.

The funeral home was in Woodvale, and Frankie parked in the car park next to Woodvale Priory. In a nearby playground housewives watched their kids as they clambered over climbing-frames and screamed down slides. It hadn't been a playground when Frankie was a kid.

He was just locking his car when he saw Daniela hurrying across the car park towards him. She came up to him and said, 'Better get back inside, Frankie.'

He caught the urgency in her voice, climbed back in, and opened the passenger door for her. They drove out of the car park and left Woodvale in the direction of Earlswood Lakes. They stopped in the car park, next to fields that led to the lakes. Frankie had spent a few drunken afternoons here in his youth, a group of them turning up with bottles of wine then hiring boats for an hour. Good, carefree days. But sitting here now, carefree was not the word that sprang to mind. He felt like screaming or punching someone.

'So the bastards are waiting for me,' he said. 'I should've figured that out for myself.'

'Just one of them. The funeral director told me. He's an old friend of Stanley's. One of his assistants told him the police had been round asking questions. They found out when you would be arriving. A junior member of staff told them.'

'Bastards. They're determined to get me.'

They sat in silence for a moment, looking out over the fields. The wet grass glistened in the sun.

Daniela finally said, 'I think you'll have to let it go, Frankie. Stanley would understand. He wouldn't want you to get caught. You've done your best. You should just leave now and go back to your new life.'

Frankie nodded. He felt desperately disappointed. 'All this for nothing. What a waste of time.'

'You had to come. At least you tried.'

Frankie climbed out of the car for some fresh air. Daniela joined him. She walked over to him, reached in her handbag and pulled out an envelope.

'Here's some money, Frankie,' she said. 'I know what was in Stanley's will. It's easier if you take some now rather than waiting for things to be settled. When the house is sold I'll send some more.'

Frankie took the envelope. It was bulging with money. 'There's a lot here,' he said.

'Not so much. It's all in five-pound notes,' Daniela joked.

Frankie smiled. 'So how did he look in there? Did you get a chance to see him?'

'He looked fine,' Daniela said. 'He looked peaceful.'

'I still wish I could find the bloke who did it,' Frankie said. 'That would be something, at least.'

'Don't keep torturing yourself, Frankie. Think of the good times. That's what he would have wanted.'

Frankie nodded. 'Just like the song. For the good times.'

Daniela smiled and they got back in the Sierra.

Frankie drove Daniela back to her car and they hugged each other goodbye.

'See you in Italy,' said Daniela as she climbed out.

Frankie sat in the Sierra for a few minutes, feeling depressed, and then opened the envelope Daniela had given him. Giving it a rough count he reckoned there was about twelve thousand pounds in there. But he still felt depressed.

Jason knew something was wrong with Karl, but didn't know if he should ask him about it. After all, he'd only known him for a week. They were hardly bosom buddies.

All of yesterday Karl had stayed in his room, just drinking as far as Jason could tell, before coming downstairs for something to eat when Gator came home. The two of them had whispered in the kitchen, made a horrible-looking spaghetti bolognese, and then took it into the living room to eat in front of the television. Karl was so drunk he found it hard to shove the spaghetti into his mouth, and ended up with sauce all over his face. Jason and Gator found that quite amusing, but Karl was on edge, and eventually left the room to be sick. Then he disappeared to his room again with a bottle of wine, the booze from the party still not finished.

Jason tried asking Gator what was wrong, but Gator just said Karl wasn't selling enough cars and was nervous about it.

Jason said, Well he won't sell many cars if he sits in his room getting drunk all day.

Gator grunted. And then soon after he sauntered off to his room as well.

When Jason went into the kitchen, he found all their dirty dishes and pans in the sink. He spent the next thirty minutes washing up everything, feeling annoyed about the presence of Gator. He felt he could grow to like Karl in time, but Gator was someone he couldn't figure out, a cold human being, and probably more than a little dangerous. When he finished the dishes he went to his own room. The house was dead quiet, almost eerie, until the thunderstorm brought some noise into the place. Jason opened his balcony doors and watched the whole thing happen, welcoming the breeze blowing into his room.

Now it was nearly midday Friday, and Jason hadn't seen Karl

come down for breakfast yet. Jason had already taken two lessons, and had a couple more later, but decided to go up to Karl's room and see what was happening. He knocked on the door twice but there was no answer.

He opened the bedroom door quietly and poked his head through. Karl was lying on the bed fully clothed, curled up in a foetal position. The room reeked of booze. Jason walked over to the window, drew the curtains and opened one of the windows. Then he went to have a look at Karl. He was still breathing, which was the main thing, but didn't look too healthy otherwise. Jason wondered whether he should call an ambulance or just let him sleep it off. He decided on the second option and went downstairs again.

After lunch and another two lessons he went back to see how Karl was doing now. He walked into the room. Karl was awake and sitting up, with a bottle of red wine in his hand. The radio next to his bed was on, tuned into a news programme.

'Don't you think you've had enough drink?' Jason asked.

Karl turned his head and smiled. 'No such thing as enough,' he slurred. 'No such thing.'

Jason pulled up a chair and sat next to the bed. He flicked off the radio and said, 'What's wrong, Karl? You weren't like this a few days ago. What's happened to the happy-go-lucky car dealer?'

'The happy-go-lucky car dealer.' Karl sneered. 'What a sham that was.' He took a swig from the bottle and stared at the bedroom wall.

'Are you worried because you're not selling enough cars?' Jason asked.

Karl smirked.

'That's what Gator said,' continued Jason. 'If you're having money problems, you can pay the rent when you can afford it, if you like.'

'Fuck Gator,' Karl spat. 'I bet he didn't say he's the problem.'

'He didn't say a lot, to tell you the truth. He never tells me much at all.'

Karl held up the bottle aggressively. 'Well, he's the cause of all this. He's the one driving me under. Do you really want to know what it's all about?'

Now Jason was getting really worried, simply by the look on Karl's face. He had never seen anyone look so frightened before. 'I think you'd better tell me,' he said.

So he sat and listened in disbelief for the next ten minutes. When Karl had finished Jason leaned back in his chair and said, 'Jesus Christ.' He didn't know whether to run out of the room and scream, throw Karl out of the house, or simply call the police. Then he leaned towards Karl and took the bottle of wine out of his hand. 'I need a drink, too,' he said.

18

Dragging ten-foot clay pipes up a sandbank all day was not Phil Gator's idea of fun. The sun was beating down on him and Brian, and both were stripped off to the waist as they strained with the weight. Old Man Carroll had told them to drag up every unbroken pipe, and there must have been over a hundred of them down there. After a few hours of this Brian became so angry he picked up a large rock and dropped it on some of the pipes, breaking them, shouting over his shoulder, 'Well that's one less we'll have to bring up!' Gator found that quite amusing but Brian stopped after smashing about five. He calmed down a little and got back to work. As it neared four o'clock, they had still only brought up about twenty pipes. It would be a long ongoing job.

'You've got a fine physique,' Brian said between breaths, as they struggled with another pipe. 'Did I ever tell you that?'

The slope was about twenty feet up, and Gator had to pull the pipe with one hand and grab on to a piece of earth with the other to get some kind of grip. More often than not the two men would slip farther back down than they had just pulled up.

'You told me that on my first day,' Gator said, 'and I didn't much care for it then, either.' The sweat was dripping constantly down his face, but he didn't have a spare hand to wipe it off.

'I want to run my hands all over your muscles,' Brian said.

Gator laughed at that. 'You're a twisted fucker,' he said, looking down the length of pipe at Brian, who laughed back at him. 'When do we get a tea break?' he asked.

'What kind of tea break did you have in mind?' Brian said.

Gator shook his head. 'The normal kind.'

Brian looked disappointed. 'Let's take one when we get this mother to the top.'

So ten minutes later they were sitting on the edge of the tarmac, out of breath, their feet dangling over the edge of the sandbank. Brian had his flask of orange juice out and they passed it back and forth. The orange tasted sweet and cool. Just what Gator needed.

'Does your wife fix your juices for you?' Gator asked.

'She does but she doesn't get them flowing.'

'You've got a one-track mind, did you know that?'

'It's all down to you. You've given me a taste of the unknown. Now I want more.'

'Well, you won't get it today. I'm too bloody knackered.' He wished Brian would get off the subject of sex and was starting to have a few regrets about what they'd done the day before.

He was saved from any more of Brian's clumsy flirting by the sight of Old Man Carroll coming across the tarmac towards them. In a few minutes he was standing behind them, out of breath from the hundred-metre walk.

'How is it progressing?' he asked Brian.

'It's hot and slow work, sir,' Brian said over his shoulder, slipping easily back into foreman mould. Gator wondered how Carroll would appreciate his foreman if he'd heard the conversation of a few minutes before. Most likely die of shock. But, then again, Carroll had been in the army, and had probably seen a bit of that kind of action himself.

Brian stood up and wandered away with Carroll, talking over the situation. Gator leaned his head back and let the sun dry off some of the sweat. His nervousness returned now that he'd stopped working. He wondered how many more days out in the sun he would have left. No doubt soon he would be banged up in some terrible remand cell in Brixton, or another shithole. Jesus, it was too depressing to think about.

Then Brian and Carroll were wandering back over and standing behind him again.

'What are you doing tomorrow, Phil?' Brian asked.

But Gator was one step ahead of them. 'Coming back here, no doubt, to pull up some more of these pipes.'

'You don't mind?' Brian said.

'What else do I have to do on a Saturday?' Gator said. If it kept his mind off other things it might be a good way to spend his day off. 'Do I get time and a half?'

'Of course,' Mr Carroll piped up. 'No problem there.'

'You're on then,' Gator said. He just hoped Brian wouldn't spend the whole day flirting with him.

After having a few drinks with Karl, Jason relaxed a bit and thought the whole thing through. They decided the best course of action was to get Karl sobered up and then get him out of the house for a while: an extended holiday, away from Gator. Somewhere in the West Country.

Jason sat in the living room and listened to the sound of the shower in the bathroom above. He went over and over the moral questions, to make sure he was doing the right thing. He was letting someone go who had been involved in a robbery that had led to the killing of three innocent people. Could he live with that? Did he really believe Karl hadn't been involved in the killings? The answer to both questions was yes. Karl was basically a simple guy, a bit thick at times, and obviously with a criminal streak in him, but Jason didn't think he was a killer. Karl wasn't tough enough for that. But he could believe Gator was. He had something cold about him, those dead eyes, and that hard streak he had seen in various nutters in his life, usually drunks in local pubs who were so inebriated they didn't care whom they hurt. But Gator had that look when he was sober, and that was even scarier.

Yes, Jason would stick by his decision, and then put the next part of his plan into action.

He heard footsteps coming down the stairs, and Karl walked in

152

looking clean and at least a little more alive than he had an hour before.

'Better?' Jason asked.

'About as good as I'll ever be.'

Karl was dressed in clean jeans, trainers and a Tottenham football shirt with Hewlett Packard emblazoned on the front. Jason didn't know much about football, but he thought shirts with sponsors' names on were about the most ridiculous things around.

'Let's load up your car and get you going,' he said.

Killing time in the Station Hotel, reading another Elmore Leonard novel, this one called *Bandits*, Frankie Bosser was startled when the telephone rang. He walked away from the window where he was sitting and picked up the receiver. 'Hello?' he said.

It was Jason. 'I need to talk to you about something. Can you come over to my house?'

'No worries,' said Frankie, catching the urgency in Jason's voice. 'I'll be there in ten minutes.'

Frankie was glad to be getting out of the hotel. It was past six o'clock and he had been reading for about four hours. Much as he liked Elmore Leonard, there was only so much reading he could stand in one day.

Jason's original plan had been just to call the police, tell them the whole story, and get them to come and stake out his house for Phil Gator's return. He had changed his mind at the last moment, though, and decided to ring Frankie. Frankie was a bit of a criminal himself – why else would he be staying at the Station Hotel under a false name? – so maybe he would have other ideas about how to proceed with the situation, and also might know whether Jason needed a lawyer. He waited impatiently in the living room for Frankie to arrive.

*

After listening to Jason's story Frankie let out a deep breath. 'It seems to me,' he said, 'you've got yourself a slight problem.'

'What's the problem?' Jason asked.

'Letting Karl go,' Frankie said. 'I think you should've walked out of the front door and gone straight to the police. They could've come round and picked him up and then waited for Gator.'

'But Karl's innocent.'

Frankie shook his head. 'He only held three people at gunpoint while the robbery was being carried out. Then he left that psycho alone with those three people. If you think that's OK, I think you've got your priorities a little screwed up.'

'I never thought of that.'

'I wish you'd called me earlier. You might well be in the shit yourself now. But nothing a lawyer can't get you out of. They'll just slap your wrist and leave it at that. But your name will be in the paper. And it could harm your career. You might find you don't get any lessons for a while.'

'Shit.'

'Do you know what they did with the guns?'

'Karl said they got rid of them.'

'Well, that's one smart thing they did. Let's go upstairs and search their rooms. Maybe we can manufacture something to get you out of this.'

They searched Karl's room first and found the money from the robbery in a box under the bed. Frankie counted it. There was just over a thousand pounds there.

'Did Karl tell you how much they got?' Frankie asked.

'Just over three thousand.'

'So Karl's probably taken some with him, or they've spent some already, or Gator's got some in his room. Let's go and have a look.'

They went down the hall and walked into Gator's small room. The only thing inside belonging to Gator was his rucksack which sat on the floor. Frankie picked it up and emptied it on to the bed.

Jason felt nervous just being in Gator's room. The casual way Frankie emptied the contents from the rucksack and then spread them on the bed made his heart beat just a little too fast for comfort. He looked at his watch and was even more worried to see the time creeping towards seven o'clock. Didn't Gator finish work around six? Wouldn't he be home soon?

'What's up?' asked Frankie.

'I think Gator will be coming back soon. I'm sure he finishes work at six. Believe me, he's not the kind of guy who'd be too reasonable if he caught you going through his things.'

'Relax,' Frankie said. 'He won't have any guns on him. Just two fists. I can take care of myself, believe me.'

Jason watched as Frankie went through Gator's personal papers. He eased open the bedroom door so he could hear any sounds of Gator returning.

'Well, well, well,' Frankie said.

Jason watched as Frankie unwrapped what looked like an old rag to reveal a pistol. Frankie held it in his hand, trying it out for size. Just the sight of it sent a shiver down Jason's spine.

'So they got rid of the guns, did they?' Frankie said.

'That's what Karl told me,' Jason said. 'Maybe that's another one.'

'Maybe,' Frankie said.

Jason was wishing now that he'd just called the police immediately. Frankie was right, he should've let them sort out the mess. But he had felt sorry for Karl and thought he deserved a break, but now he had implicated himself. And what Frankie had said about his lessons was true, too. If he got his name splashed all over the local paper, it wouldn't take long for his lessons to dry up. Why hadn't he thought of that? Why the hell had he got involved in all this? He should've stuck by his gut reaction the

155

first time Karl had come round to see the house, trusted in those original doubts. But no, the thought of some rent money had outweighed common sense, and now look where it had got him. The line of an old folk song came to mind: 'Now see what your love for money has done,' or something like that.

Frankie was leafing through some photographs. Jason just wanted to get out of the room and run from the house, jump in his Mini and drive away until Gator disappeared from his life for ever.

'Has he just come back from holiday or something?' asked Frankie.

'Pardon?'

'This Gator. Has he just come back from holiday? Have a look at these photos.'

Jason stood next to Frankie and had a look at the snaps. At first he didn't recognize the person in them, but then saw it was Gator, with long hair and stubble.

'Now that you mention it,' Jason said, 'he has just come back from Europe. He was out there hitching for a while. A few months I think. He came back a couple of weeks ago, or something like that. He's still got a tan.'

'That's interesting,' Frankie said.

'What is?'

'I'll tell you later.'

Now Frankie was putting everything into the rucksack, stuffing it in with no respect, not caring how it all went back. Gator would know for sure it had been tampered with.

Jason said, 'Shall I go and call the cops now?'

Frankie threw the rucksack back on the floor and looked at Jason with anger in his eyes. He picked up the gun and now Jason was scared of him, too.

'No,' Frankie said. 'I think we'll wait for Gator to come home.'

19

At seven o'clock on Friday evening Jesse Morgan was having supper in Nicola's flat. She had made her usual salad, lots of avocado and tomatoes, and there was another bottle of wine, opened, which Morgan had so far ignored. He was due back at the incident room in an hour to follow up more leads, and drink was the last thing he needed. The incident room had been working round the clock since the murders, but still there was a whole load of nothing leading nowhere.

'It must be very frustrating,' Nicola was saying. 'Don't you ever get worried that a crime won't be solved?'

'All the time.'

'The pressure must be horrendous for the men in charge.'

'It is. The trick is not to let it get to you. If it gets to you, who knows what might happen?'

'Like fabricating the evidence, you mean?'

'That sort of thing. I've seen it happen.'

'Not in Woodvale, surely?'

'Not on the same scale, no. I saw more of it in London. It's like any other job, really. Those that want to succeed will make things up to get noticed, tell the odd lie here and there. Only in police work the consequences are a lot more serious.'

Nicola looked appalled. 'Have you ever done it?'

'Not that I know of,' Morgan said, disappointed that she would have to ask that of him. He took a sip of water. 'There are a lot of honest cops around,' he said. 'It's the corrupt few that get the bad press for the rest. It's like football hooliganism: the minority tarnishing the majority. Can we talk about something else?'

They talked about country music and the Red Lion. Nicola told some amusing stories about chat-up lines that various men used on her in the pub. Morgan found himself getting jealous.

When they'd finished eating they went into the main room and lay on the bed together fully clothed. They kissed and rubbed against each other but Morgan didn't want to go any further because he was running out of time. He told Nicola he wanted their first lovemaking session to be uninterrupted and not against the clock. She reluctantly agreed. He lay on his back and looked out through the windows at the trees on the priory. As his hour ticked slowly by he could feel his spirits dropping. When his time was up he climbed off the bed.

Back at the incident room in Orton he leafed through computer printouts and handwritten messages at one of the desks. Ian Kiddie had gone for his break, no doubt taking Spotless for a walk, so Morgan exchanged information with Mulligan, who was sitting at a desk in the corner, going over some paperwork, a steaming cup of coffee in front of him. His face looked white and tired, strained, the face of a man fighting a losing battle. He glanced up at Morgan.

'I've got more paper than the *Sunday Times*,' Mulligan said, 'and none of it means a fucking thing.'

'I know what you mean,' Morgan said. 'I think we're fast approaching the stage where we need a lucky break.'

'Didn't we pass that stage yesterday?' Mulligan rubbed his eyes and stretched. 'I need some sleep. About a week of it.'

'Why don't you go home? Kiddie and I can take care of things. If anything important comes up we'll give you a ring.'

'Are you sure?'

'Positive. Go home and reintroduce yourself to Faye. See if your kids still recognize you.'

Mulligan's face brightened. The thought of home was obviously too tempting. He stood up and started getting ready to leave.

After lodging a message for Kiddie with the supervisor Morgan went outside and climbed into his car. He headed back into Woodvale and drove slowly round the streets. He knew where he was going but didn't want to get there too fast, wanted to savour the feeling of doing something useful. If this hunch went nowhere, he didn't know what he'd do next. Eventually he came to the street he wanted and parked outside Mrs Gator's house.

When the working day had finished at seven – an extra hour to haul up a few more pipes – Phil Gator had been so tired he couldn't face the walk to Redgate for the bus back home. He should've asked Brian for a lift, but instead found himself heading for the nearest pub, walking stiffly down the rutted road and off the industrial estate. He turned right towards Merstham and walked into the Bricklayer's Arms, a pub he had been in before, one he knew wouldn't mind a bloke in dusty clothes looking like he'd just been in an argument with a cement mixer. He sat at the bar and had a pint of bitter with a cheese and onion roll. That went down so well he repeated the dose twenty minutes later. Then he topped it off with another two pints.

While he was drinking there was a darts match going on in the corner. With his fifth pint in his hand he turned to watch them, a group of men and women his age laughing and joking like they had no cares in the world. Gator envied them. Feeling a little more alert now, he slid off his stool and walked over when the game finished.

'Do you mind if I score the next one?' he asked, walking over to the blackboard and picking up the chalk. The group didn't look too pleased by his presence, so he flashed his best smile and they reluctantly agreed. That meant he would play in the next game.

Four of the group started throwing: 501 straight in. Gator had always been lousy at subtracting darts scores, and with the beer making his head spin he was soon making mistakes. The players started laughing at him and had to call out their scores, which he dutifully wrote down. He began wishing he had stayed on his stool, but then one of the girls came over and stood next to him. She smiled kindly and said, 'You look like you need help.'

For the rest of the game she told him the scores, standing quietly at his shoulder, almost whispering them to him. Gator found her voice so soothing he felt he could go to sleep on the floor right there as long as she kept talking to him. He looked at her now and then when the others were throwing. She had short dark hair, an odd-looking face, with no chin and a large nose. Not the sort of girl he would go for.

But when the game was over, and he found himself partnering her for the next game, he soon changed his opinion. Because now he could see her body.

She had a lovely slim figure, her tight blue jeans fitting snug on her backside, a sight Gator could hardly take his eyes off. She was wearing a white shirt over a white T-shirt, no bra as far as Gator could see and not that much breast, but he knew such things could be deceptive. She said her name was Sue. Gator replied, 'How do you do,' and Sue said she hadn't heard that one before.

They lost their game in no time, Gator throwing darts all over the place, once hitting the scorer off a rebound. Everyone else laughed, but the scorer didn't look too pleased.

Gator and Sue went to sit at a table, and he bought her a Bacardi and Coke while he sipped on his sixth pint, but who was counting? He felt better than at any time since the shooting on Wednesday. Hell, it was Friday night, he was in a pub and he was chatting up a girl he thought he had a chance of pulling. What better way could there be of spending an evening?

They talked gibberish to each other for the next hour, the meaningless meandering of drunks. It was all good fun to Gator. Eventually they got round to important matters, such as could he stay at her place for the night? Sue nodded but said the only problem was that she lived with her mother. Gator said, well so do I, and they both laughed.

They left the pub before the others and walked down the road towards Merstham. It took them about twenty minutes and Gator had to stop on the way for a piss. He found the most expensive car on the street, a white Mercedes the size of a tank, and pissed all down the driver's door. 'A white Merc doesn't belong in a street like this,' he said. 'It deserves to be pissed on.'

Sue laughed, standing right next to him, looking at his dick. Gator liked her forward approach and thought tonight would be a certainty, no doubt about it.

When they came to Sue's house she led him in quietly and sat him on the living-room sofa while she went to make coffee and toast. Gator read a *TV Times*.

Sue came back with a tray full of toast and steaming coffee. She put the tray on the floor and asked Gator if he'd like to hear some music. Gator said he didn't care one way or the other. Next thing he knew Sue had put on a Pink Floyd album and he was wishing he had said no. She sat at his feet and ate two pieces of toast with raspberry jam. Gator did the same. He found himself sobering up a little but tiredness was setting in and his mood didn't improve as Sue started talking about her boyfriend. Then she was saying how she still fooled around a little, seeing as how her boyfriend lived in Liverpool. Gator perked up again.

A little while later, she was sitting on the sofa next to him and they were kissing. Gator got his hand up Sue's T-shirt and started fondling her breasts. That went on for a while before he tried for the promised land, but as his hand went down lower she caught hold of it and shook her head. 'This is as far as I go,' she said.

Gator felt let down. 'How about a quick hand-job?' he asked, moving her hand to his jeans.

Sue pulled her hand away. 'No! I don't do that either.'

'So, by having certain rules, you don't feel guilty when you next see your boyfriend?'

'That's right.'

'And you think he does the same?'

'That's what he tells me.'

'I think he's having you on.'

'Maybe. But I have my own standards.'

Gator couldn't be bothered arguing about it. Normally he wouldn't give in so easily and would stay up all night trying to get his way. Then he started thinking that maybe he should just rape the bitch as he was going to go to gaol anyway. Go out in a blaze of glory. He would still like to see that arse of hers, bent over in front of him. He looked at the clock on the mantelpiece and it said twelve-thirty. He rested his head on the back of the sofa to think about it and closed his eyes.

The atmosphere in the incident room had picked up, ever since Jesse Morgan had walked back in and told them all about Phil Gator. Then he had phoned Mulligan and dragged him away from his wife and kids. Mulligan hadn't minded; he was so relieved to get a lead at last. Now he was pacing round the room, organizing people, looking at information on computers, trying to get some sort of idea where Gator had disappeared to. Morgan watched from a desk, eating a cold kebab. He was feeling pretty pleased with himself and thinking he might even go home in a minute to catch up on some sleep. Let someone else do some legwork for a change. Ian Kiddie was sitting opposite, watching with disgust as Morgan ate.

'I don't know how you can stand those things,' Kiddie said. 'Who knows where that meat came from.'

Morgan looked at him in disbelief. 'This from a man who eats haggis on a regular basis.'

Kiddie didn't have an answer to that one. He had only just come into the room, having been at home for dinner and taking Spotless for a walk.

'So how did you extract all this information from Mrs Gator?' Kiddie asked, changing the subject.

'I just went in and sat talking to her for a while,' Morgan said. 'The softly, softly approach. When I'd shown what a good guy I was I let her have it between the eyes. I told her I didn't believe her earlier story and she broke down in tears. She spewed up the whole thing. She said her son had just come back from a three-month trip to Europe, had obviously got into some sort of trouble, and had moved out of her house. He told her not to tell us anything, didn't even tell her where he'd moved to. She can't even make a guess where he is. She doesn't know much about his personal life. I think she's scared of him.'

Kiddie nodded. 'But he doesn't have much of a track record. You really think he's one of the killers?'

'They all have to start somewhere. I think he's been progressing towards something like this. I mean, I'm not definite about it, but I've got a hunch.'

Kiddie smiled. 'Yeah, you're looking pretty smug.'

'Some of us have it and some of us don't,' Morgan said.

Just after one o'clock Jason rubbed his eyes and said he was going to bed: 'I don't think I'll be able to sleep but I'm going anyway.'

Frankie said, 'Just relax. There's nothing to worry about. If you hear any shooting, it'll only be me.'

Jason looked at the gun in Frankie's hand. 'I can't believe all this is going on. It's like a bad dream.'

Frankie knew a bit about bad dreams. That had been exactly how he'd felt the night he'd shot the policeman.

Jason said, 'I won't say goodnight because I don't think it will be.'

Frankie was glad when Jason stopped whining and left the room. Now he was alone with his thoughts, sitting on an armchair he had pulled around to face the front window of the living room. He would see anyone walking up the garden path to the front door. See that fucker Gator come in, lead him to the living room at gunpoint and ask him some questions. Like, was it him who killed his father when he arrived back from Europe with his rucksack? Then just put the gun to his head and blow him away. It wouldn't be too hard. When he had shot that policeman three years ago he'd found it remarkably easy. Once you got used to the noise and the kick it was not such a hard thing to pull a trigger. And he'd be doing society a favour this time. They wouldn't have to lock up a triple murderer. Save the taxpayer a bit of money. Hell, they should give him a reward for it. Bounty Hunter Bosser. Like that Steve McQueen film *The Hunter*, the last one he made before he died on 5 November 1980. One of the few dates that Frankie remembered. The day he lost interest in going to the movies.

He looked at his watch in the dark. It was now after two o'clock. Where the hell was the bastard?

20

When the door to the living room opened, Phil Gator finally woke up. He was lying on the settee, sun coming through the curtains, and there was a middle-aged woman standing above him. It took him a few seconds to realize where he was.

'What are you doing here?' the woman said in an angry voice. 'Get your feet off my sofa!'

Gator reluctantly took his feet off the settee and sat with his head in his hands. 'I'm a friend of your daughter,' he said, not looking at her.

'My daughter doesn't bring people back here without my permission. Now kindly leave my house!'

Gator stood up and pushed himself at the woman. She backed away with a scared look on her face. He put one of his large hands round her throat and pushed her against the fireplace. He liked the look of fear he was generating. 'Why don't you shut the fuck up,' he said. The woman was probably in her fifties, and had quite a good figure. Grey hair. Gator had never had a grey-haired woman before. He reached up his left hand and started squeezing her right breast. The woman started struggling, tears coming into her eyes. Gator felt himself getting excited, but at the same time he couldn't be bothered. He let the woman go and left the room.

Walking down the street he passed a church with a clock and saw that it was after eleven o'clock. He remembered then that he was meant to be at work at nine to pull up some more of those bloody pipes. He walked in the direction of Redgate and the industrial estate. He might as well see if Brian was there and if anything was happening.

*

Frankie Bosser woke up in the armchair at about the same time. He swore to himself, and went upstairs to see if Gator had come back in the middle of the night. He checked on Gator's room but it was empty.

He walked back down the hall and knocked on Jason's door. He entered and saw Jason lying in bed reading a book.

'Did Gator come home?' Jason asked.

'No,' Frankie said. 'Maybe he's done a runner. I fell asleep eventually. Armchairs were not made for sleeping in.' He rubbed the back of his neck as he walked to the window and then out on to the balcony. After looking at the view and breathing some fresh air he came back in. 'You've got a nice house here,' he said.

'Nice but expensive,' said Jason. 'Sometimes I wonder if it's worth it.'

'Your own house is always worth it. Everyone needs roots. Somewhere to come back to.'

'You sound a little homesick.'

'I want to get back to Italy. I suddenly feel like a stranger here. What book are you reading?'

'*No One Here Gets Out Alive*. A biography of Jim Morrison and the Doors.'

Frankie hoped that wasn't a prophetic title. 'I've been reading a lot of Elmore Leonard since I came here,' he said. 'You should try him. A crime writer.'

'I don't read crime novels.'

'They can be entertaining if you get the right one.'

'They still don't appeal. I enjoy American writers, though. Modern ones.'

'You'd like Leonard then.'

'But I'm not interested in crime.'

'You're mixed up in one now. You might find yourself growing to love it.'

'I doubt it.'

Frankie pulled up a chair and told Jason about his father, and how he thought it was Gator who had killed him. Jason found the whole thing unbelievable but Frankie eventually managed to convince him. He told him about the rucksack connection, how his father had been killed by a traveller, and how Gator – or at least Gator in the holiday snaps – fitted the description that Joe had given Frankie in the Railway. Jason agreed there were a lot of coincidences.

'I'm going to go back to the hotel to freshen up,' said Frankie. 'If Gator comes back, I want you to give me a ring at once. All right? I want to ask him some questions before we call the cops. I'll take his gun with me as well. So he can't use it on you.'

'Thanks.'

'Only joking.' Frankie left the room and walked outside to his car. He was looking forward to a shower and then a few hours' sleep.

As Gator walked towards the Portakabin, he saw Old Man Carroll over by the edge of the yard where the pipes had slid into the quarry. Probably watching Brian struggle on his own, thought Gator. The old codger. But when he reached Carroll's side and looked down he couldn't see Brian at all.

'Sorry I'm late,' Gator said without conviction. 'I was so knackered from yesterday I overslept.'

Carroll turned and stared at him, making him feel about as welcome as a migraine.

'It doesn't matter anyway,' Carroll said. 'Brian rang to say he won't be coming. One of his children is ill. I tried to ring you but your mother said you hadn't been home.'

'Stayed at some friends',' Gator said.

Mr Carroll was dressed casually today: black slacks, a dark blue shirt and a cream cravat. Gator thought he looked like a ponce.

'I may as well go home, then,' Gator said. 'I can't drag them up on my own.'

'Indeed,' Carroll said.

167

Gator turned to go but Carroll said, 'The police were here looking for you today. I told them you were meant to be working, but it didn't look as though you would be turning up.'

Gator froze and then glanced quickly towards the Portakabin to see if there was anyone hanging around. He turned back to face Carroll who was still looking out over the drop.

'What did they want to see me about?' he asked.

'They didn't say,' Carroll said. 'In some trouble are we?' He looked at Gator with a superior expression on his face.

'What's it to you?' Gator said.

'Oh, it's nothing to me,' Carroll said. 'You mean nothing to me at all.'

Gator stepped towards Carroll and stood directly in front of him. His face was about six inches away. That grey moustache and that stupid cream cravat. He thought back to a couple of weeks before and to the old guy whom he'd hit because he'd splashed him. All these pensioners were getting on his nerves. Why were they so cocky? Did they really think they could take on someone like him? 'It's just as well,' he said, 'because you mean nothing to me either.'

Then he put both hands on Carroll's shoulders and pushed him backwards over the edge.

Ian Kiddie had been left by Jesse Morgan to keep an eye on the Ellis Pipes builders' yard. But he had drunk a lot of coffee that morning and after hanging around near the Portakabin for two hours he had to go for a pee. If he had not been on duty he would've just done it behind some pipes, but being a man of standards he had walked into the office, asked Mr Carroll where the nearest toilets were and was told they were quite a trek. He had to head in the direction of the factories; the toilet was just outside a warehouse.

When he got back to the Portakabin about five minutes later he looked through the window to see if Mr Carroll was there but the place was empty. Kiddie wandered into the yard and started searching for the old guy. He decided to have a look at the far side, where Mr Carroll had said there'd been a landslide and he'd lost some of his stock. He walked over to the edge of the tarmac and looked down at the broken debris below. Then he saw something else. He said, 'Oh shit,' and reached for his radio.

Gator heard police sirens as he was walking back towards Redgate. He jogged quickly down a side street so the cops in the passing police car wouldn't see him and watched as the car whizzed by, heading in the direction of the industrial estate. He thought it was probably for something else, but it was no time to take chances.

When he reached Redgate High Street he walked quickly among the Saturday morning shoppers towards the train station. He got a few unusual looks from passers-by, and had to agree with them that he probably looked a bit of a mess. He was still dusty from the previous day's work, more unshaven than usual, and his short hair was dirty and spiky. Not the sort of sight you would want your dear little children to be confronted with on a harmless morning's shopping trip. But Gator had far bigger worries to occupy him.

He walked up to the row of taxis at the station and climbed into the back of the first one in line. 'Naughton Road in Woodvale,' he said to the driver.

The driver looked in his rearview mirror and said, 'A little politeness wouldn't go amiss.'

Gator reached over the back seat and squeezed the driver's neck. 'Don't give me any lip,' he said quietly, dropping a ten-pound note on to the passenger's seat. 'Now get this chariot moving, I've got things to do.'

The driver squirmed out of Gator's grip, looked at the ten-pound note on the seat next to him, and started up the taxi.

Down in the basement at Naughton Road Jason was finding it hard to concentrate on his only lesson of the day. As soon as

Frankie had left the house he had started getting nervous about the return of Gator. What he really wanted to do was pick up the phone and get the police to come round and take care of it all right now. But Frankie had said he wanted to talk to Gator first, and as Frankie seemed to know more about these things than Jason did he had gone along with him. For now at least. But he had decided that if Gator didn't turn up by the end of the day, he would ring Frankie and tell him he was going to call the police. After all, what difference would that make to Frankie? The guy who had killed his father would still end up behind bars.

So Jason tried to concentrate on the lesson but couldn't. About halfway through he left the basement and went upstairs to get a glass of wine. He filled another glass, too, and took them both downstairs to Barry, his long-haired, Neil Young lookalike pupil. They sat and talked and drank, and Jason said he could have the whole lesson for free.

And about twenty minutes later he heard the front door open.

Standing in the hall, Gator listened for sounds in the house. Then he walked upstairs and went into Karl's room. It looked a little emptier than the last time he'd been there, but he couldn't figure out why. He went down on his knees by the bed and pulled the box out from underneath. There was still some money in there, so he took it all out and stuffed it in a pocket.

He walked down the hall to his own room and pushed open the door. He noticed the rucksack lying on the floor, not in the place he had left it. He picked it up hurriedly and turned out the contents on to the bed. Someone had been through it. And, worst of all, his gun had disappeared.

Feeling the anger welling up inside, he left his room and walked into Jason's. No one there either. Where the fuck was everyone? Then he thought of the basement. That's where Jason always was. He was sure to be hiding down there.

*

When Jason heard Gator stomping around upstairs he felt like running straight out of the house. But he'd been a coward all his life and felt it was about time he stood up to one of these hooligans for a change. So he started writing on a piece of manuscript paper and handed it to Barry.

'You've got to do me a big favour, Barry,' he said. 'Leave your guitar here, go to the nearest phone box and ring this number. Ask for Terry Elliott and tell him to come and see me straight away. That guy who just came in is bad news and I'll need some help with him.'

Barry said OK, but looked worried as hell.

'It's all right. Just do as I say,' Jason dug in his pocket for some change. 'Here's some money for the phone. The nearest one's up near the off-licence. When you've done that just go home. I'll ring and explain later.'

Jason walked Barry to the door that led into the garden and they waited until they heard the cellar door at the top of the stairs open. Then Barry slipped out as Gator came thumping down the stairs.

'I knew I'd find you down here, you little shit,' Gator said, marching across the floor and pushing Jason hard in the chest. Jason fell backwards over a chair, his glasses falling to the floor, and smashed into a guitar that was leaning against the wall. Gator pulled him to his feet, grabbed him by his shirt collar and pushed him against the whitewashed wall.

'Now tell me who's been in my room,' he said, 'and tell me where Karl is.'

Jason was so scared he could hardly speak. 'Karl's gone,' he managed to say. 'He left yesterday.'

'Oh yeah? And where did the chickenshit go?'

Gator's face was about an inch away from Jason's. All goatee, stubble and bad breath.

'He wouldn't say. Just grabbed his stuff and went. I saw him going in your room, though.'

'The sneaky bastard,' said Gator and relaxed his grip.

Jason thought he was in the clear but then found himself being shoved towards one of the chairs.

'Sit there and don't move,' said Gator.

Jason watched him walk towards one of the amps and pull out a lead, one of Jason's new ones, twenty-four quid's worth. Gator approached him with the lead and started tying him to the chair. He wrapped it around Jason's body, his hands behind his back. Jason looked over at the guitar he had fallen against. His beloved black, limited-edition Takamine. The neck was broken. That would cost plenty to fix.

When Gator had finished tying him up he came round and stood in front of him. 'Now, I've got a few things I have to do, and I don't want you going anywhere. If you're a good boy, I might even untie you before I go. But first of all I'll give you a little reminder, so that you won't even think of fucking with me.'

Then he was behind Jason, who felt rough hands reaching for his. His right thumb was suddenly in Gator's grip and he started bending it backwards. Jason could hardly believe this was happening to him, and his body went rigid as he waited for what was coming next. He heard his thumb crack, and then a very loud scream coming from his own throat, a scream so unusual that he didn't think it had emanated from him but from some kind of animal.

But when the pain hit, he knew that the scream was all his.

21

Standing at the top of the landslide with Ian Kiddie, Jesse Morgan looked down on the policemen below as they zipped Mr Carroll into a body-bag, strapped him to a stretcher and then started hauling him up the slope.

Morgan shook his head. 'Jesus, Ian. Why didn't you just have a piss behind a stack of pipes?'

Kiddie was looking mortified. He knew now that if he'd remained on the scene, Gator would be theirs. Morgan felt sorry for him and there would be some awkward questions to answer later. In the space of a few days Kiddie had been outwitted by Frankie Bosser and now, through carelessness, by Gator. Superintendent Cole would want to know why.

'I honestly didn't think he'd turn up,' Kiddie said. 'I'd been waiting for two hours. Besides, maybe the old man just fell down.'

Morgan looked at him with annoyance. 'I think you're grasping at straws there.'

'You should've left someone with me. It would've taken two of us to handle Gator anyway.'

'Funnily enough, someone else was on the way. I thought of that when I got back to the station. It took them over two hours to get here, though. That's not going to look too efficient either.'

'A balls-up all round then.'

Morgan took Kiddie by the arm. 'I'll buy you a cup of coffee in that canteen. See if anyone there saw Gator.'

They walked down the dusty road to the canteen. There was a small gathering of factory workers along the route and several of them asked what was going on. Morgan told them the old man had fallen down the slope.

When they were in the canteen Morgan bought two cups of coffee. He asked the man behind the counter if he had seen anything unusual that morning, anyone who shouldn't be on the premises. The man thought for a moment, scratching his sandy hair, and then nodded his head.

'Now that you mention it, there was something unusual.'

Morgan was all ears.

'I saw this bloke jogging past. He looked like he was in a hurry. I know him by sight. He comes in here most lunchtimes. Works for the builders' merchants. But they don't work Saturdays so I couldn't figure out why he was here.'

'What did he look like?' Morgan asked. Kiddie had moved closer to his side.

'He was wearing a green T-shirt and jeans. Covered in dust. Looked a mess.'

'What about his face. Did he have a beard?'

'Yeah. One of those little ones. One that every young bloke and his dog seems to have these days. And short hair. Cropped. He's a tough-looking bloke. Never says much when he comes in here. I've never liked him much. Sort of person you dislike on sight.'

Morgan took a sip of his coffee and looked at Kiddie. 'Do you still think the old man just fell over?' he said.

Frankie Bosser was just stepping out of the shower when he heard the telephone ring. He picked it up and a hotel clerk put through the call. After listening to the panicky message from one of Jason's pupils, he dressed quickly in jeans, T-shirt and trainers, and left his room on the run.

He took the stairs two at a time, walked quickly through the hotel lobby, then sprinted towards his car in the car park. It was only when he was halfway to Woodvale that he realized he had left the gun back in his hotel room.

*

Gator was in Karl's room looking for car keys. He had decided to do a runner, something he should've done a few days ago. He had just had a quick shower and put on some clean jeans and a T-shirt. He almost felt like a new man. He hadn't bothered to shave. He would let the full beard grow back again to confuse people.

He eventually found some keys in the middle drawer of the dressing table, under a pile of underpants. There were two sets and he put them both in his pocket. Then he went downstairs with his rucksack.

He walked out of the front door, and swore when he saw that Jason's Mini was blocking in the blue Nissan. The Fiat was still in the garage. After marching back into the house, Gator took Jason's keys off the hall table, returned to the drive and moved Jason's car. He left the Mini, unlocked the Nissan's door, threw his rucksack on to the back seat and was about to climb in when he realized he'd left the robbery money in the pocket of his dirty jeans. He swore again and went back inside.

Running up the stairs, swearing, Gator went into the bathroom where he'd left his jeans in a pile on the floor. He took the money out of the pocket and was about to leave when, through the open window, he saw a car pull up outside. A blond bloke got out and walked quickly up the front path. Gator hadn't seen the man before, but he looked tough, and that was enough to set the alarm bells ringing.

Frankie saw the front door was open, as was the door of the car in the drive. It looked as though someone was getting ready to leave.

He walked into the house and shut the front door quietly. He flicked the safety latch on the lock and put the chain on as well. Not much of a deterrent, but it would slow Gator down for a few seconds if he tried to make a run for it. Then Frankie started searching the ground-floor rooms.

*

Standing completely still in the bathroom, Gator figured that the man must be an undercover cop. He had that cop look about him: short hair, strong physique, the right sort of height. Who else would be coming to the house at this time of day? He didn't look like a guitar student.

He started thinking of his options. There was no way he could run out of the house, back the car out of the drive and get away. He would have to confront the bastard, either kill him or knock him out. He looked around for some kind of weapon. There was nothing in the bathroom: every razor in the cabinet was a safety. He crept out along the hall towards Jason's room. Karl's was slightly nearer but he couldn't recall seeing any heavy blunt objects in there. Maybe Jason had a spare guitar he could swing above his head. An electric one would be good. They had some weight in them.

As Frankie crept up the stairs he was wishing he hadn't left the gun back at the hotel. It would've been so easy just to point the thing and get a confession out of Gator. In his present situation, though, he knew he would just have to hit first and ask questions later. He hoped he had the strength to take on the guy. He was fit from all his skiing through the winter, and he'd done enough push-ups to last a lifetime these past few weeks, but fitness and fighting were two different things. He was willing to bet Gator was used to having the occasional brawl, whereas Frankie's last fight had been . . . when? He couldn't remember.

He reached the top of the stairs and the first doorway was on his left: Jason's room. He took a step to the right so he would be some distance from the door and then turned and rushed into the room.

Gator didn't expect someone to come flying through the doorway and it took him by surprise. He was armed with a section of a microphone stand, and already had it raised when he saw the blond man heading straight for him. But because the bloke was

176

moving so fast, he didn't have time to take proper aim or put all his strength behind the stroke. Plus the guy had his arm up, as if he expected some sort of blow. The microphone stand slammed down on his attacker's left arm, and then Gator saw a right fist coming towards his face.

Frankie caught him a good one and was pleased to see Gator had dropped his weapon and was falling backwards on to Jason's bed. He picked up the microphone stand and swung it at Gator's head, catching him on the jaw. Gator's eyes glazed over. Frankie stood back and waited for the next attack. He wanted to keep his distance. If he got into a clinch he thought Gator might squeeze the life out of him with that big pair of hands. Jesus, they were like baseball gloves.

Lying slumped on the bed, with a dizzy head and double vision, Gator was thinking maybe he'd met his match. He had a fleeting urge just to give in to the situation, hand himself over to the cop and accept the consequences. Then the thought of prison came into his head, and there was no way he wanted to return there. But what really drove him back to his feet was the prospect of going back to prison for the rest of his life knowing that the last person he'd fucked was a man. No. That was too depressing to contemplate. He wanted just one more woman before being caught.

With the microphone stand raised and ready, Frankie knew he was in control of the situation. It was a groggy Gator who got to his feet and came for him, and Frankie let rip with an almighty Botham swing. The stand shuddered in his hands when it made contact, and Gator stumbled away, through the windows and on to the balcony. He stood against the railing, looking at Frankie with confusion. Frankie dropped the microphone stand and marched out to face him.

He grabbed Gator by the throat and pushed him hard against

the railing. Gator just looked at him, blood running down his forehead from the last blow.

'Now cast your mind back,' said Frankie, 'to the events of two weeks ago. You punched an old man who was sitting in his van outside a pub. Does that sound familiar?'

Gator shook his head.

'Does that sound familiar?' said Frankie again.

Again Gator shook his head.

Frankie was beginning to have doubts. Maybe Gator hadn't been the one after all. 'You punched an old man,' he continued, 'and later on the old man had a heart attack. That man happened to be my father, you miserable fucker.'

But still Gator didn't respond. Frankie loosened his grip slightly so Gator could breathe a little easier. Perhaps his grip had been too tight for Gator to talk. He stood back ready for another attack, not knowing what to do next.

Then Gator looked Frankie in the eye and started smiling. 'The old guy,' he said breathlessly. 'Yeah.' He nodded. 'That old bastard who splashed me with his van. Now he was one fucker who deserved to die.'

'What do you mean, splashed you with his van?'

'I was walking down the road and he drove right by a puddle and splashed me. A mean-spirited thing to do.'

So that was what this was all about. A stupid accident with a puddle. Frankie knew his father would never do something like that intentionally. He knew a few people who would, though. And this Gator was definitely one of them.

Frankie took another step back, then lashed out with a right-hander, putting everything into it. Gator flipped backwards over the railing and fell on to the patio below. Frankie looked down and saw his crumpled body, more blood coming out of his head now, spreading across the stones. He rested his arms on the railing and wiped the sweat off his forehead.

He pointed down at the body and said, 'Gator, gotcha.'

22

Frankie found Jason down in the basement, still tied to the chair, dried tears on his face, his right thumb bent back at a terrible angle. He untied him while Jason cried some more. Frankie couldn't tell if it was from relief or pain. He helped him out of the chair and said, 'Let's get you to hospital.'

'Where's Gator?' Jason asked.

'Out on your back patio,' Frankie said. 'Taking in some sun.'

He took Jason out to his car and told him to wait a minute. Then he went back into the house, through to the patio, and knelt down beside Gator. He found the money in one of Gator's pockets and took it downstairs to the basement. He stuffed the money inside the hole at the front of the broken black guitar. Jason wouldn't find it until he got the guitar fixed, and by then he would've answered all the cops' questions, but wouldn't have been able to tell them where the cash was. The cops would have to write it off as lost money.

Back in the car, Frankie drove quickly towards Redgate General. 'I'll drop you off at Casualty,' he said. 'If you can make up some lie about how you broke your thumb, that would give me some time to get away. Just tell them you fell down the basement stairs or something. Then, when you get back home you can call the cops and tell them the truth. Leave out the part where you delayed ringing them, though. Just say Gator came round and you were worried so you rang me. You'll have to tell them where I was staying, so I'll be checking out as soon as I get back. The main thing is to fabricate it a little so you don't get into any trouble. You don't have to mention your conversation with Karl.

As far as you're concerned he just disappeared. You'll be in the hospital a few hours. That'll give you a chance to work out your story. OK?'

'So you want me to tell them all about you?'

'I'd be pleased if you would,' said Frankie, and then he told Jason about the real reason he had left England three years before. 'If they know I caught a triple murderer, it could work in my favour in the long run. I'm not going to hang around to find out, though. There's nothing to keep me in England now. I've got my life in Italy to look forward to.'

For the rest of the journey Frankie told Jason about his fight with Gator. Jason wanted to know all the details and Frankie caught the respect in his voice.

'It's nothing to be proud of,' said Frankie. 'Any arsehole can fight with his fists. You just stick to your music. That's a lot more creative.'

Jason climbed from the car as it pulled up outside Casualty. He was in a lot of pain and couldn't get in there quick enough. The two men shook left hands and Frankie said he'd be in touch. But he knew he probably wouldn't.

Back at the hotel Frankie gathered together all his things and stuffed them in his suitcase. He left the Elmore Leonards on the night table – he'd read four of them – and went downstairs to pay his bill.

He left the suitcase in the Sierra and walked over the road to the Home Cottage. In the saloon bar he found the person he was looking for and sat down next to him.

His name was Tommy, and he'd been a regular in the Home Cottage for as long as Frankie could remember. He was a gangster from the Kray era who had retired to Redgate. Frankie didn't know much about him, but he had always been a little scared of him when he'd worked at Fuller's Earth in the seventies. He would walk into the bar after a shift, and there would be Tommy, always in the same seat, a few cronies sitting around him, hanging on his every word. The man had an aura about him, that hard look that all criminals have, that don't-give-a-shit, I-rule-the-world attitude. Frankie had never liked him, but now it was time to use him, to get some information out of him.

Tommy was on his own, an old man in his late seventies with a softer look to his face now. That's what Frankie disliked about most gangsters. Once they reached old age they tried to come across like harmless good-old boys, tried to make out they hadn't been all that bad in their youth. But Frankie knew for a fact that Tommy had once put an axe through someone's head; he had read about it in a true-crime book once. And there were lots of other things he had done, too, things Frankie didn't know anything about, things Frankie would prefer not to know anything about.

Tommy looked at Frankie with a puzzled expression. 'Do I know you?' he asked.

'My name's Frankie Bosser. I killed a cop once.'

The name took a few seconds to register, then Tommy's right hand came out for Frankie to shake. In the old days Tommy had been a big man, six feet tall and wide in the shoulders, but slumped in his chair he seemed shrunken by age. Still had all his hair, though, dyed a ridiculous black.

'I remember.' Tommy nodded. 'Then vanished to Europe. What have you been up to all these years?'

'Just getting by,' Frankie said. 'But I'm in a bit of a pickle now. You'll be able to read about it in the local paper. I need to get out of the country fast. I need a plane. Do you know anyone who can fly me out?'

Tommy sat and thought about it, took a sip of beer, then reached in an inside pocket of his blazer. He took out an address book and started flicking through it. 'Now, let's see who we can find,' he said.

Frankie went to the bar and bought an orange juice and some

cigarettes. He returned to the table and sat down with a lighted one, the smoke relaxing him a little. The first one he'd had since killing Gator.

'Here it is,' Tommy said. He reached in another pocket and brought out a notebook with a small pen attached. He wrote down two names and two numbers, ripped out the page and handed it to Frankie.

'One of those should be able to fix you up,' Tommy said. 'But it'll cost you.'

'I've got the cash,' Frankie said, knocking back the orange juice in one. Killing someone was thirsty work. 'Thanks a lot. I've got to be going. The posse will be on my trail any minute.' He winked at Tommy.

'Don't let them catch you. Good luck.'

They shook hands and Frankie was out of there, looking for the nearest phone box.

He found one just outside the train station and dialled the first number: no answer. The second number connected and a voice said, 'Yeah?'

'I need to speak to Billy Cracken,' Frankie said.

'Who needs to speak to him?'

'My name's Frankie Bosser. I got this number from Tommy—' but Frankie couldn't remember what Tommy's surname was. 'Tommy in Redgate. I forget his last name.'

'Tommy in Redgate. Yeah, I know him. How is Tommy? Still dyeing his hair?'

Frankie laughed. 'Black as black can be.'

'That's my Tommy. What did he give you this number for?'

'I'm on the run from the police. I need to get a plane out. He said Billy could fix me up. He said he's the man who makes things happen.'

'Nice of Tommy to say that. Well, this is Billy speaking. You need a plane to where? France?'

'France would be perfect.'

'No problem. But it'll cost you. Four grand. Three for the pilot, one for me. You've got that kind of money?'

'I've got the cash on me now.'

'What did you do, rob a bank?'

'Well, I killed a cop a while ago, and that's why they're after me.'

'Way to go, Frankie.' Billy chuckled. 'Now here's what you have to do. Have you heard of Lydd airport?'

'Yeah. Down on the coast. Near Ashford.'

'That's right. Just drive down there and ask for a man called Simmonds. He's the pilot we use. Give him the four grand and he'll fly you to Outer Mongolia if you ask him nicely.'

'That's great,' Frankie said. 'Thanks a lot.'

'No problem,' Billy said. 'Any time. Cop killers are always welcome here.' He chuckled again and the line went dead. Frankie left the phone box and headed back to the hotel car park.

The drive down to Lydd took over an hour and a half. Frankie joined the M25 at Woodvale, headed east towards Sevenoaks, then joined the M20 going south. When he reached Ashford he had to get on the A2070 and that took him most of the way. He had never been to Lydd before, but was familiar with the South Coast from his Eurobooze days. He knew Lydd was virtually on the sea and it would just be a short flight across the Channel.

Frankie reckoned that Jason would've told his story to the cops by now, and the police were probably sending messages to all the major airports to look out for him. They would hardly contact Lydd, though, and Frankie felt confident that he was virtually home and dry.

The airport was well signposted, and Frankie pulled on to the road leading to it, flat fields all around, not too many buildings. The airport itself looked like a ghost town: empty hangars and rundown buildings, not a soul around.

Frankie parked in front of what looked like the main building and walked in. There was a canteen on the right, and tables and chairs on his left near the window, looking out on to the runways where rows of private planes were parked. There were a few housewives sitting at the tables with prams and groups of kids running around. Frankie couldn't see anyone of importance to talk to, though, so he walked up to the canteen counter and asked the lady there for the pilot called Simmonds. She gave him directions.

Frankie had to go back outside and cross the parking lot towards another building. He pushed his way through some swing doors, and entered what had once been a plush bar: crimson carpet on the floor, built-in seating, tables screwed to the floor. It was all unused now, though, and Frankie had to step over a dead seagull on the floor. He wondered how such a place could be allowed to go downhill.

He heard the sound of a TV and saw a group of men smoking and watching cricket in a room at the back. They directed him to yet another building when he asked for Simmonds. Frankie left the way he had come in, picking up the dead seagull on the way, and laying it outside on the grass.

He walked over to a two-storey office building and pulled open a stiff door that scraped the floor as it moved. The other pilots had told Frankie that Simmonds had moved into the first-floor offices and turned them into a flat. After a flight of wooden stairs, Frankie knocked on a door. There was no answer so he pushed it open and entered. The room was full of junk and furniture, like someone hadn't unpacked all their belongings yet. Another room to the right was just the same. He could hear lovemaking sounds coming from the room on his left, though, and headed that way, saying hello in a loud voice.

The lovemaking room was a lounge, with a sofa and armchair, a small glass coffee table and a window that looked out over a flat roof and then the airstrip beyond. There was a hi-fi unit and TV next to the window. A sex video was in full flow on the TV. Frankie stopped to watch a little: explicit stuff he'd never seen before.

He started looking in the other rooms and soon found the main bedroom with a man lying asleep on the double bed, an empty bottle of wine on the bedside table. Frankie walked up to the man and shook him awake.

'Mr Simmonds?' he said loudly a few times. The man woke up after several shakes and looked at Frankie.

'Who are you?' he asked.

'My name's Frankie Bosser. I got your name from Billy Cracken. He said you could fly me to France. I've got some cash for you.'

The man's eyes lit up and he struggled into a sitting position. 'Well, why didn't you say so? I could do with some money, get me out of this stinking hole. Only problem is we can't go until tomorrow. They're doing some repairs to my plane.'

'Can't we use another plane?' asked Frankie.

Simmonds looked up at him. 'This isn't like a minicab service. It's my plane or nothing.'

Frankie was disappointed. He wanted to get out of the country immediately. But he knew he didn't have any other options.

'So what time in the morning can we leave?' he asked.

'As soon as the sun comes up,' said Simmonds.

'Can I crash here tonight?'

'Of course,' Simmonds said, 'but crash is not a word we use around here.'

'Sorry.'

'You can sleep on the sofa. Get some drink in. Watch some blue movies if you want.'

'No thanks,' said Frankie. 'They're not much good unless there's a woman around.'

'Tell me about it,' said Simmonds.

23

Jason spent most of Saturday afternoon and evening at Woodvale police station. They put him in an interview room and a man called Mulligan asked him questions. Then a man called Morgan took over. There was another policeman called Mills hanging around, and Jason was getting very confused by all the different names beginning with M.

He managed to get a lawyer to sit with him, a large man called Lawrence who was recommended by the solicitor he'd used for his house. But Lawrence was a cigar smoker and, with Mulligan's cigarettes, the interview room was soon about as healthy as some of the clubs Jason had to play in. His clothes were starting to stink, his hair felt dirty, and his broken thumb was aching like mad. He just wanted to go home and crawl into bed.

They drove him home just after eleven o'clock, still not completely satisfied with his story. But Jason had fixed it all in his mind while he'd been at the hospital and he now almost believed the fabrication himself.

He had changed Frankie's version of the story slightly: Frankie had been at Jason's house when Gator came home; they had talked and Gator had let it slip that he'd punched a man who'd splashed him a few weeks ago, a man who turned out to be Frankie's father; Frankie had then fought with Gator and thrown him off the balcony. Jason had left out the part about ringing Frankie at his hotel; that way he could say he didn't know where Frankie was staying and that would give him longer to get away, although Jason presumed he was long gone by now. He said he didn't know anything about the triple murder, but the police tied

Gator in with it for definite when they found the red Fiat in the garage. And now they were out looking for Karl as well. Jason had reluctantly given them a description of him. He still felt sorry for Karl, and hoped they wouldn't find him.

And now Jason was back home, taking a long hot bath, a tumbler full of red wine balanced next to him. He was thinking about a lot of things, but mostly of how he was now in exactly the same position he had been in a fortnight before: living in a house he couldn't afford and without a lodger. The only major difference was that he now had a broken thumb and a broken guitar. He couldn't bear the thought of advertising for a lodger again. So where did his life go from here?

After thirty minutes in the steam, Jason climbed out of the bath and towelled himself down. He walked naked from the bathroom into his bedroom, put on some boxer shorts and stepped on to the balcony to breathe in the night air. He looked at the drop that Gator had experienced. Not too far, but far enough to crack open a head. The patio was still sealed off with blue and white police tape.

Jason wandered across the hall to Karl's room, turned on the light and spent a few minutes poking around his belongings. He wouldn't throw anything out just yet. It would be best to wait for Karl to be caught and then see if he made contact. Would Jason go and visit him in gaol? He thought not.

He stood by the window and looked down at the garden: the hedges still needed a trim, the grass a cut. With a broken thumb, though, he doubted that he could do any of that.

He was about to go back to his room when he glanced to his left and saw the blue Nissan sitting in the drive. Why the hell was that still there? But, then again, why the hell shouldn't it be there? Jason felt the excitement in his stomach. The police had probably thought the car belonged to him. And who was to say at this very moment that it didn't? He could either sell the car for three or four grand or keep it instead of Heather's Mini. Tell her to take it to London. Cut the last tie between them.

All of a sudden the future didn't seem so bleak. Jason smiled to himself and left the room. He would go outside and lock the Nissan in the garage before anyone noticed it.

It was one o'clock on Sunday morning before Jesse Morgan finally got away from the police station and over to Nicola's flat. Now he was lying fully dressed on the bed while Nicola was naked next to him, but covered by a single sheet. Morgan was sipping a can of Carlsberg Special Brew and trying to unwind, trying not to think too much about Nicola's naked body.

'So you went round to the guitarist's house and found Gator lying on the back patio?' asked Nicola.

'Lying in a bloody mess,' Morgan said. 'Thrown from the balcony above by none other than our old friend Frankie Bosser, the elusive pimpernel.'

'I'm sure I'm missing something here. Can you slow down and explain in detail?' Nicola turned on her side to face him. He stroked her bare arm with the same fingers that earlier in the day had been touching a dead man.

Morgan told her the events of the day according to Jason Campbell, a story that was full of holes as far as he was concerned, but what did it matter? Phil Gator had been caught and that was the main thing. Karl Spoiler would be picked up within a week, unless he was a whole lot smarter than they thought. The local and national papers would get their story, and in a few days the whole place would return to normal.

'And what's going to happen to you now?' asked Nicola. 'Promotion for finding the killer?'

'Who knows?' Morgan shrugged. 'Who cares?'

'You don't mean that.'

'Oh, don't I?'

'You love it really.'

'Oh, do I?'

'Yes, you do.'

'Oh no, I don't.'

'And what about Ian. Is he going to get into trouble?'

'I shouldn't think so. What can they do? Reprimand him for taking a piss?'

'For leaving his post.'

'I don't think so. They might slap his wrist but that's about it.'

Morgan got off the bed and walked over to the window. He drew back the curtains and looked out towards the priory but he couldn't see much with the lights of the room still on. He finished his can and turned around.

'Why don't you take your clothes off and come to bed?' Nicola said.

'Sounds like a good idea,' Morgan said, setting his can on the TV. At last it would happen.

He stripped off to his underpants and climbed into bed. They snuggled up to each other and Morgan could feel himself becoming aroused. He broke off for a second and said, 'You know what amazes me?'

'What?'

'This whole chain of events was triggered by Gator punching Stanley Bosser because he splashed him. Just one pathetic little splash. Don't you find that a bit worrying?'

'Not necessarily. Gator and Karl still would've gone to the post office and killed three people.'

'But Frankie Bosser wouldn't have come into the picture, would he?'

'No, he wouldn't.'

'This job never fails to surprise me. Maybe that's why I stick with it.'

They kissed and Nicola said, 'Umm, that's nice. You should think of a way you can do it more often.'

'I'll try my best,' said Morgan.

'I'll be back in a minute,' said Nicola, climbing out of bed and walking to the bathroom. Morgan watched her naked figure disappear. He couldn't wait for her to come back.

He stretched out and closed his eyes. The beer had gone straight to his head and he felt extremely tired. How would he perform in bed after such a long time without any practice? Would it be like riding a bike?

A deep wave of sleep crept over him. He couldn't fight it and he let himself go and was transported to dreamland.

On Sunday morning Frankie Bosser woke up early to the smell of bacon and eggs frying. He got stiffly off the sofa, where he'd suffered a bad night's sleep, and pulled open the curtains. It was light outside and the clock on the video said ten past six.

He walked down the hall to the toilet in boxer shorts and T-shirt, said good morning to Simmonds who was in the kitchen, already fully dressed. Frankie relieved himself, splashed water on his face, and then joined Simmonds.

'Orange juice in the fridge,' said Simmonds. 'Breakfast coming up in a few minutes.'

'You'll make someone a lovely wife,' said Frankie.

'That's what I intend to do.'

They had spent the previous evening listening to music in the living room, telling each other their life stories. Frankie had rung for a pizza, and Simmonds had drunk a bottle of wine with his pizza. He was a good looking man, but had the appearance of someone who drank too much: red face, skin starting to go blotchy, drinker's belly. Frankie was told about the downhill spiral Simmonds's career had taken, how he had been a pilot for British Airways for ten years until he'd got the sack for too much drinking. After years of unemployment he had got the job at Lydd airport, but his wife and two kids lived nearly five hours' drive away, so he only saw them on occasional weekends. Now he'd had enough. With the three thousand that Frankie had given him, he would pack it all in and go back to his wife, find a job – anything – that would keep him by her side.

The two of them had talked until midnight, Frankie asking Simmonds about his kids, wondering whether it was time he tried having some of his own. Now that his father was dead, he was the last in the line of Bossers. It would be nice to think that someone else was following on behind him. He would need to find a woman first, though. Maybe he could get together with Veronica when he returned.

They made small talk over breakfast, Frankie itching to be on his way but not wanting to hurry Simmonds. He sensed the pilot liked his company.

Eventually Simmonds stood up, patted his stomach with satisfaction and burped. 'Let's go,' he said.

Over the Channel, with the sun shining through the cockpit window of the small four-seater plane, Frankie Bosser was thinking anything was possible in this life. He was feeling good about himself, good about life, for the first time in two weeks. Next to him, Simmonds was shouting out a fragmented conversation, flying the machine with ease, despite being hung over. Simmonds had reassured him before take-off that flying a plane drunk was easier than driving a car drunk, because there was hardly any traffic and certainly no pedestrians. Frankie found that argument hard to contest.

'When I get back,' Simmonds was saying, 'I'm going to park this thing and never fly again. You should feel honoured to be my last passenger.'

'I am,' Frankie said.

'Then I'm going to drive home and stay with my wife and kids for ever. I don't give a fuck about anything else any more. My family comes first from here on in. They're the only things that are worth a damn. A man isn't complete without his family. You know that, don't you?'

Frankie nodded. He looked over at Simmonds, a man slightly younger than himself, a man with his own problems, trying to work them out. In another life they could be good friends, Frankie thought.

He looked off into the clouds and thought of Veronica again. They would sit down when he got home and see if they could

191

work something out. He was glad to be heading back to Italy, and didn't mind the thought that he might never see England again. If he had failed by not seeing his father before they put him underground, at least he had found his killer. And he had also sorted out for now which country he wanted to live in.

He smiled to himself as he saw France in the distance. Soon they would be landing and he could hop on a train to Italy.

Pointing out of the window, he shouted to Simmonds, 'Frankie Bosser comes home!'